"Why do you have to act so high and mighty?"

"I suppose I may seem that way," Brendan replied dryly, "if you're used to weaklings like Tom Maynard. Why don't *you* act your age and stop wallowing in self-pity?"

Ingrid had had enough of Brendan's telling her what to do. "No more sermons, please. You may have saved my life but you don't own me, Brendan Kavanagh!" She gathered her belongings to board the plane. "Starting now, you'll be able to forget all about me."

Ingrid's voice was steady, concealing the sharp pang of misery in her heart. She knew she should have been glad to be going home at last, but the thought of never seeing this unpredictable man again was one she couldn't bear!

Books by Madeleine Ker

HARLEQUIN PRESENTS
642—AQUAMARINE
656—VIRTUOUS LADY
672—PACIFIC APHRODITE

These books may be available at your local bookseller.

For a free catalog listing all titles currently available,
send your name and address to:

Harlequin Reader Service
P.O. Box 52040, Phoenix, AZ 85072-2040
Canadian address: Stratford, Ontario N5A 6W2

MADELEINE KER

KER

pacific aphrodite

Harlequin Books

TORONTO • NEW YORK • LONDON
AMSTERDAM • PARIS • SYDNEY • HAMBURG
STOCKHOLM • ATHENS • TOKYO • MILAN

Harlequin Presents first edition March 1984
ISBN 0-373-10672-6

Original hardcover edition published in 1983
by Mills & Boon Limited

Printed in U.S.A.

CHAPTER ONE

As she drifted out of the darkness of her long sleep, she could still hear the murmur of the surf. But her pains had receded. The crawling fire of sunburn had become a dull warmth around her shoulders and across her face, and the bruises and abrasions which covered her body were numb. She was lying on her side, with her knees drawn up protectively and her hands clasped under her face. That was the position she had chosen to die in.

She floated dreamily in a state of not-quite-awake peace, simply grateful not to be in pain. Slowly, though, she began to realise that the murmur she could hear was not the surf after all, but the voices of two men speaking quietly at her bedside. She lay still, her eyes shut tight, and tried to concentrate her fuzzy senses on their conversation.

'. . . a dreadful ordeal, at any rate,' someone was saying. 'The whole thing's a complete mystery.'

'Is there nothing familiar about her at all?' asked the second man, whose voice was deep and authoritative.

'Nothing,' sighed the other. 'She definitely doesn't come from these islands.'

The other man grunted. 'I'll take her on to Fiji, anyway. She needs hospital treatment.'

'Poor child,' said the first man sympathetically. His voice was light and pleasant. 'She's only about sixteen, isn't she?'

'Older than that,' said the other man. It was a dark voice, she decided dreamily, a midnight blue voice. 'I undressed her and washed her as soon as I picked her up and got her on board. And she's definitely not sixteen. I'd say she was about twenty-one or two.'

A puny spark of anger flickered in her. Who had undressed her, seen her body so intimately and nakedly exposed? Someone took her wrist, and strong fingers bit into her pulse. There was a measured pause. Then the deep voice said, 'Fifty-three. Still weak, but a lot better.'

'Poor little mite,' said the man with the lighter voice. 'Where on earth can she have sprung from? Maybe she was on holiday somewhere on Fiji, and got washed off the beaches?'

'It's five hundred miles from Fiji,' said the deep voice sceptically. 'That's a long way to drift in a catamaran.'

'It's thirteen hundred to Australia,' pointed out the other, 'and a lot farther to New Zealand.'

She lay quiet, her mind wrestling tiredly with what they were saying. This conversation wasn't making any sense to her at all.

'In any case,' the dark voice concluded grimly, 'she'll tell us when she comes to.'

'Was there nothing with her to identify her?' asked the man with the lighter voice.

'Just this,' said the other. She felt something tug at a thin chain around her throat.

'Well, that's something,' said light-voice. 'What is it—an initial T?'

'Yes. The trouble is, it may be someone else's initial—her boy-friend's, for instance.'

'It's most likely hers,' said light-voice thoughtfully. 'Tracey? Trixie?'

'She doesn't look like a Trixie,' said the midnight-blue voice drily.

'No, she doesn't,' agreed the other. 'Poor kid, you can see she was very pretty.' A finger touched her cheek lightly. 'Will that skin ever heal?'

'It's hard to say,' said the midnight-blue voice indifferently. 'Young skin is amazingly resilient. And the doctor on Fiji will know how to treat her. But she's been badly sunburned all over. Look.' The covers lifted away from her shoulder, and it was all she could do to stop herself from curling up in pain and shame.

'Oh dear,' said the light voice, sounding sick.

'It's not pretty,' agreed the midnight-blue voice calmly. The covers drifted gently back into place. 'It could heal completely. Or she could be scarred for life.'

'You don't seem to care,' said the other man.

'Saving this little life has cost me precious days, Josh. I don't want to get involved with her—I'm simply going to hand her over to the hospital on Viti Levu and be on my way.'

'But you are involved,' the other man pointed out.

'Look, Josh—I have to deliver *Seaspray* to Collins by the thirteenth. I simply can't afford to be held up.'

'Anyway,' said the other, and there was a note of pity in his voice, 'she's lucky to be alive.'

'She should be dead,' agreed the midnight-blue voice callously. 'And when she wakes up, she may wish she was.'

She couldn't help it. A tear crept from under her swollen lids, scalding her raw skin. The man with the light voice muttered something, and there was a silence. Then something soft dabbed her cheek, and the light voice said quietly, 'You're going to be all right, dear. Just relax.'

'Let her sleep, Josh,' said midnight-blue voice calmly. From first to last, he had spoken without pity, almost without feeling. She heard the door close, and opened her swollen lids fractionally. Through blurred eyes she could see a tiny bedside table, walls of polished wood, an oval window, rimmed with neat brass. A bright orange lifejacket hung behind the door. A boat. She was on a boat. As she drifted back into the shadows, she tried not to cry any more. The salt tears burned her skin too much for relief.

The cool trickle against her lips was sweet, and she swallowed greedily; then choked as some of the liquid went into her windpipe. Coughing weakly, she put out her hand to thrust the cup away. She could taste orange-juice, sweet and acid.

'Take it easy,' said the midnight-blue voice. She was sitting up, supported in his strong arms. She opened her eyes blearily to see whether his eyes were midnight-blue to match his voice. They were grey. She surveyed his blurred face uncaringly, then opened her mouth for more juice. As she drank the nectar, she closed her eyes again, feeling the sweet coolness spread through her tired body. When he pulled the cup away, she was weakly indignant.

'More,' she croaked.

'These will help.' He put the bitter pills on her tongue, and commanded, 'Swallow.'

They felt as big as marbles in her inflamed throat, but she swallowed nonetheless. Her reward was more juice. But half-way through drinking, she began to feel so tired again that she couldn't hold her head up, and it lolled forwards, spilling orange-juice down her chin and over the sheet. The midnight-blue man tried to hold her up, but she was past caring. The soft darkness was waiting for her, maternal and loving, and she began to slide into it with relief.

'Don't go to sleep yet,' he said urgently. 'Where do you come from? What's your name?'

As she floated through the shadows to the very bottom, she tried to tell him her name; but her lips wouldn't move.

When she awoke again, it was night. She lay for a long time in the darkness, slowly becoming aware of new discomforts—hunger and thirst. She rolled the sheets back with drunken care, and tried to swing her legs over the edge of the bunk. They felt like someone else's legs, heavy and useless. She pushed them over, and they hit the deck with a thump. Her head was beginning to ache again. With an effort she sat up. The world stopped, spun the other way for a few seconds. Knowing she was going to collapse back, she heaved herself to her feet, swaying like an axed tree, and collapsed heavily over the tiny table. At once, all the pains leaped out of the shadows with razor teeth, and she retched. Footsteps descended the companionway quickly.

'God,' he muttered under his breath. She clung to him weakly as he helped her back to her feet. 'What the hell are you doing out of bed? Get back in!'

'Going to be sick,' she croaked. 'Fresh air—please!'

He paused. 'Come on then—but just for a few moments. And go easy.'

She clung to his strong arms as he helped her up the companionway and on to the fresh darkness of the deck. The wind was cool on her fiery skin, and the night was brilliant with stars. He sat her down in the cockpit, draping a blanket over her knees, and put a cold metal bowl into her hands.

'Use that if you want to be sick,' he told her. She nodded, and lay back with closed eyes, waiting for the long tides of nausea to resolve themselves one way or the other. At last she felt better, and she opened her eyes again. He was a tall, dark figure looming over her.

'Where am I?' she croaked.

'You're on the *Seaspray*,' he told her. 'I'm taking you to Fiji.'

'Fiji?' she asked with numb astonishment. 'What—why Fiji?'

'Because there's a hospital there,' he said drily. 'Isn't that where you come from?'

'Fiji?' She stared at the dark figure. 'I don't even know where it is!'

There was a silence. Then he came to sit next to her.

'How are you feeling?' he asked.

'Terrible,' she confessed. 'My back and face are in agony. And I'm afraid I'm very confused. What am I doing here?'

'Don't you remember?' he asked quietly. She shook her head, huddling herself into the blanket. He took a chart out of a compartment next to the wheel, lit a small Tilley lamp, and spread the map out on her knee. In the flaring white light the chart seemed to be mostly sea, dotted with innumerable islands. He put his finger on one of them.

'That's where I found you,' he informed her. 'Hunter Island.'

She stared at the map in growing bewilderment. Something was terribly wrong—only she didn't yet know what it was. Perhaps she was still dreaming? But no, the lancing agony of the sunburn across her back told her she was wide awake.

'I don't understand,' she stammered. 'What's Hunter Island? Is it in the Channel?'

He stared at her in surprise, the white light reflected in his level grey eyes.

'The Channel? What Channel?'

'Why the English Channel, of course,' she said in alarm.

'The *English* Channel?' He pointed to the map. 'Hunter Island is just off the Tropic of Capricorn, a few hundred miles off New Caledonia—between Australia and the Fiji Islands.'

A deep horror had begun to settle over her, and she gazed at the map with unseeing eyes.

'But—but—I've never been there in my life!'

'Look,' he said patiently, 'you're still confused. But people are going to be looking for you everywhere. Can't you give me a name, someone to contact on your behalf?'

She sat mute, slowly beginning to understand what was so terribly wrong. Her memory. She couldn't remember *anything*. 'Where are your family? They'll be looking for you. Your parents will be desperate by now.'

'I haven't got any parents,' she said dully.

'Well then,' he said patiently, 'what's your name?'

Dear God, she couldn't remember. She racked her mind desperately. 'I—I don't know,' she said miserably.

'You don't *know*?' His voice was astonished. 'Where did you set out from?'

'I don't know,' she said, terror rising in her.

'Don't be silly,' he snapped. 'Where were you staying before you landed up on Hunter Island? Fiji? Australia?'

'I don't know,' she said, trembling. He drummed his fingers on his knee angrily, saying nothing. 'I swear to God I don't know,' she repeated shakily.

'How can you say you don't know?' he asked angrily. 'You can't have forgotten.'

'But I have. I've forgotten everything.' She began to cry, letting the bowl slip on to the deck with a clatter.

'Stop blubbering,' he said shortly. 'Try and think— where did you set out from? Don't you remember the red catamaran?'

'I don't even know what a catamaran is,' she said through her tears. 'I can't even remember my name!' She was sobbing violently by now, and he helped her to her feet.

'You'd better get back into bed,' he said, more gently. 'You've had a tough time. You'll remember everything when you've rested a bit. Come.'

As he eased her into the bed, she clung to his arms in sudden panic.

'For God's sake don't leave me,' she begged.

'I'll just be up on deck,' he smiled, but she refused to let him go.

'Don't leave me alone,' she pleaded. 'Sit with me until I fall asleep. *Please*. I'm so frightened!'

'There's nothing to be frightened of,' he said patiently. 'I'm going to give you two more pain-killers.' She swallowed the pills obediently, and lay back, holding his hand tightly. 'We'll be in Fiji by dawn,' he told her quietly. 'I've radioed the hospital in Viti Levu, and they're waiting for you. It's a beautiful island. You'll like it there.'

He tried to disentangle his fingers from hers, but she clutched at his hand.

'Don't go,' she whispered fiercely.

He sat with ill-concealed impatience, waiting for her to sleep. As her eyelids flickered closed, her mind's eye held the image of his face—grey-eyed and strong, with an authoritative, passionate mouth. But she didn't stop crying, quietly and persistently, even when her body had relaxed into passivity, and her scratched hand had uncurled to release his fingers. He stared at the burned face, shook his head in irritation, and went back up on deck.

The hospital at Fiji was small and cool. She could see coconut palms through the window of the little room they had put her in. The brown-skinned nurses had washed her hair and dressed her wounds. They had also given her a mirror to study her face in. It was a pale, oval face, with livid pink patches of raw skin on her cheeks and nose. But it was, thank God, a familiar face, with full lips and wide green eyes. Her body was badly sunburned as well; the sun had stripped the satiny skin away like a blowlamp on a painted door. Her body, too—slender-legged and graceful—was familiar, though she had never seen it looking so thin. Even her breasts, normally full and impudently tilted upwards, were smaller. And painfully burned. There were still traces of pearly-pink nail-varnish on her fingernails and toenails. The nurses cleaned these off and painted the nails again with a clear lacquer. Her shins, which seemed to have been hacked and cut somehow, were especially painful.

But nothing else was familiar. Nothing at all.

Sometimes she felt waves of terror, which made her tremble violently; but nothing helped. As soon as she tried to project her mind back, to recollect the past, it was as though night had descended over her thoughts. As though she had run into a brick wall in the dark. There was simply nothing there. All she could remember was the man in whose arms she had awoken.

The silver chain was in a saucer next to her bed, and she had picked it up three or four times, studying it intently. She remembered nothing about it—yet someone must have given it to her. Or perhaps she had bought it herself. The initial T that dangled brightly on the end tantalised her. T—what? One of the nurses had sat with her, and they had run through every name they could think of beginning with T. Nothing. She couldn't even know whether she would recognise her own name if someone said it.

The more she thought about it, the more terrifying her predicament became. Who was she? Where had she come from? And, perhaps most frightening of all, what sort of person was she? How very strange, she reflected, was this thing called *me*. Identity, personality, mind, soul—they were all such vague, and yet such important things. What had she lost?

At the moment, she knew, she was as pure and innocent as a new-born child. She had done no one wrong, committed no crimes. Yet in the past—no, she corrected herself, in *her* past, there might lie untold horrors. Or untold wonders. Supposing, for instance, she had been in love with someone before her loss of memory. Where had all that love gone? Was it stored up inside her, waiting to be released? Or had it simply been erased, the way you erased the music on a cassette tape, the good with the bad?

What was more, she faced another prospect—that of actually recovering her memory—God willing. What then? Would she, in the interim, have adopted a new personality, a new identity? Would she always be the same person inside? Or would she, when the locked gates of memory once opened, be confronted with a new self, a new identity that would be her own—and yet not her own?

It was like a nest of Chinese boxes; once you opened one, another appeared. You could go crazy trying to work it out! In desperation, she had turned to the doctor for guidance.

'You just relax,' the little Fijian had told her kindly. 'It will all come back to you. The specialist is coming over from one of the other islands this afternoon—he'll be able to do more for you than I can.' And they had dressed her blistered skin again.

'Where is he? The man who brought me in?' she asked anxiously. 'What's his name?'

'His name is Brendan Kavanagh,' the doctor had smiled. 'He'll be in soon—just relax.'

The nurses had left her with a huge pile of magazines to look through in an effort to jog her memory, but flicking through them soon made her dizzy, so she just lay back on the pillows, waiting for him.

His face was indelibly imprinted on her mind. It was the one thing she knew for certain—a man with grey eyes and a commanding mouth, with dark hair and a midnight-blue voice, whose arms were strong and secure. Nothing else was real. And if he didn't come to her, she didn't know what she was going to do!

When he eventually came into her room, dressed in a dark sweater and jeans, she almost cried with relief. He was big, bigger than she had remembered, with wide shoulders tapering to an athletic-looking waist. He looked fit and tanned and hard. And not particularly friendly. But that didn't matter.

'Thank God you're here,' she said weakly, marvelling at him.

'Hullo,' he said, dropping a bunch of flowers into her bedside vase, 'Any luck yet?'

She shook her head sadly. 'Nothing at all.' She took a deep breath. 'It seems that you saved my life, Mr Kavanagh, whatever happened to me.'

He shrugged. 'It's the first rule of seamanship to rescue those in need.' He picked up the silver chain and contemplated it drily. 'We're just going to have to call you Tee,' he said.

She touched the flowers he had brought her. They were strange and beautiful, and smelled exotically sweet.

'You're quite an enigma, Tee,' he said, sitting back and folding his arms. 'You've been big news since Thursday morning—three days ago. The airwaves have been buzzing with you from here to Japan. The trouble is—nobody wants you. Nobody seems to have lost a twenty-two-year-old blonde for years!'

She looked at him miserably. 'What's going to happen to me?'

'God knows,' he said indifferently. 'At the moment you're just an unclaimed piece of lost property. I don't think there's anything anyone can do until you've remembered who you are.'

She dropped her eyes to her chipped nails, utterly

depressed. She couldn't think of a single thing to say. He leaned forward and tilted her chin up with his hand.

'Tee, listen to me. This can't go on. You've landed me in a lot of bother with the Fijian authorities. They want to know where your passport is, who you are. The Inspector is coming to see you this afternoon. Please tell me—are you putting this on? Trying to hide from something?'

'No,' she said unhappily, 'I promise you I'm not.'

'Because if you've done something wrong——'

'I haven't done anything wrong,' she said hotly.

'How do you know?' he asked ironically. She glared at him. There was something hostile, abrasive in his manner which grated on her raw nerves. Couldn't he see she wasn't ready to be interrogated like this?

'I just know I haven't done anything wrong,' she said sullenly.

'Whatever you've done or not done,' he said more kindly, 'it would be a lot better to face the music. People will understand. If you've been in some kind of trouble, or if you're frightened of something—well, no one's going to be too hard on you. Just spit it out——'

'I swear I'm not lying,' she said tearfully, hurt and angry. 'Can't you understand? I can't remember anything. And I'm so frightened ——' She broke off, her eyes blurred with tears. 'Please believe me,' she choked.

He sighed, watching her with compassionate eyes.

'I didn't mean to upset you,' he apologised. 'I'm just trying to get at the truth. You told me you had no parents, back on *Seaspray*. Is that true?'

'Yes,' she nodded instinctively. 'I'm absolutely sure of that—don't ask me how I know. But I know I don't have any parents.' She brightened slightly. 'That's something, isn't it? At least that's something I *do* know.'

'It's not exactly helpful,' he grunted. 'How far back can you remember?'

She thought hard, her eyes still wet. 'I remember waking up on your yacht,' she said slowly. 'You and another man were talking about me—and I started to cry.'

He nodded. 'That was Josh Leclerque. He's a meteorologist, stationed on Conway Reef. That's where I took you first, because I thought you must have come from one of the Loyalty Islands.'

She shook her head. 'I've never heard of them.' She noticed that his eyes had dropped to her breasts, which were dimly visible through the blue nightie the Fijian nurses had given her. 'I'm not very beautiful,' she said, covering herself quickly with the sheet. 'My body looks like raw meat.'

'That's what bodies are usually made of,' he said drily.

She looked away, at the blue sky and palm-trees visible through the hospital window.

'Tell me how you found me,' she requested.

'You were wrecked on Hunter Island. You don't remember that?'

She shook her head. 'I think I remember pain, and being afraid that I was going to die,' she said slowly. 'What's Hunter Island?'

'It's mostly reefs. There's nothing on it—just sand and rock. I spotted your red catamaran lying in the shallows, so I anchored *Seaspray* and rowed the dinghy ashore. You were lying in the sand, just about to become food for gulls and crabs.'

She studied him as he spoke. He was an utterly poised, self-confident man, projecting an impression of hard maturity. Casually dressed as he was, he carried an air of authority that was almost chilling; and the level grey eyes, fringed with long black lashes, stared out at the world with imperious arrogance. It was a face which would have been almost frighteningly stern, she thought, but for the passionate curve of his mouth, and the full lower lip. It was his mouth which hinted that within this cold, hard man, volcanic passions could lurk—emotions made all the stronger and fiercer because of the iron self-control which obviously ruled his life.

'I don't think you would have regained consciousness,' he was saying thoughtfully. 'You'd probably have died later that afternoon. Maybe sooner, if the gulls had started pecking at you.'

She felt sick. It was as though he were talking about someone else, someone not remotely connected with her. Yet it had been her own body lying on that lonely reef, her own life fluttering away. He was telling her things about herself which she had no knowledge of.

'What's a catamaran?' she asked tentatively. 'Is it some kind of boat?'

'Yes. The number on the sails might have helped to identify you, but——'

'The sails blew away,' she said suddenly. He froze, watching her intently. 'I remember that,' she said with dawning triumph. 'I remember the sails blowing away!'

'When?' he asked sharply.

'I don't know. And I don't remember any red boat. But I've got this image in my mind of the sails tearing loose from the mast and blowing away across the sea.' She smiled at him, her green eyes sparkling with delight. 'I remember something!'

'Terrific,' he said ironically. He stared at her with level grey eyes for a few seconds, then glanced at the diver's watch on his wrist and stood up.

'I can't stay here all day,' he said. 'And those nurses are just about to serve your lunch.'

'I don't want any lunch,' she said in alarm. 'Where are you going?'

'I've got about fifty phone calls to make to America, for one thing,' he said coolly. 'You've got a busy afternoon ahead of you, by all accounts——'

'Don't leave me,' she said urgently.

'Don't be silly, Tee. I have to——'

'Please don't leave me here!' she said in panic.

'Oh, for God's sake grow up,' he snapped. 'You're not a child!' He turned on his heel.

'*Please!*' she implored desperately. Something of the urgency in her tone made him look back, naked annoyance in his face.

'What is it with you?' he demanded, his mouth taut.

'I'm just so frightened,' she said breathlessly. 'I don't want to lose you.'

'Dear God,' he muttered in frustration. 'Okay—if it means so much to you, I'll be back tonight. That suit you?'

'Promise,' she begged him. But he was already walking out into the corridor.

She slumped back on to her pillow, fighting back the feeling of panic at his leaving. How could he know that, to her, he was the only real thing in a terrifyingly lonely and unreal world?

The pretty young nurse who brought her fish lunch in mistook her tragic expression for worry over her burns.

'You'll get your looks back, never fear,' she beamed, plonking the plate down on her tray-table. 'Them wounds is healing already. And what pretty skin you have! I wish my skin was half as pretty.' She stood back to watch the blonde girl pick up her knife and fork with listless hands. 'Eat up,' she counselled. 'The psychiatrist is just raring to have a look at you. And after *him*,' she added solemnly, 'the Inspector of Police himself wants a turn.' She watched her patient with awed eyes. 'You sure making the news around here, my dear!'

She was exhausted and trembling by the time Brendan Kavanagh walked back into her room that evening. A light came into her eyes as soon as she saw his tall, well-made figure. He stood out from other people as though he alone had colours, and all the rest were in black-and-white. A smile flickered across her pale mouth as he came to her bedside, and looked down at her with brooding eyes.

'I hear the psychiatrist didn't get anywhere,' he said by way of greeting.

'He hypnotised me,' she told him tiredly, 'and tried to find out what my name was. But it didn't work. He said all my memories were locked up somewhere deep in my subconscious. He said it was probably a reaction to the ordeal I'd been through.' She reached out wearily and touched the flowers he had brought her. They had already begun to droop in the tropical warmth of the evening.

'What did the Inspector say?' he asked, sitting down beside her.

'He bullied me,' she said, her face twisting at the memory. 'He doesn't want me on this island. He says I should go back to Australia, because he thinks that's where I came from.' She looked at him, ready to cry again. 'The psychiatrist is going to try and get at my memory again tomorrow,' she said. 'With drugs.' The fear in her voice made him sigh, and his sea-grey eyes washed over her face with something like sympathy.

'You're scared, aren't you, Tee?'

'Terrified,' she said miserably. 'What am I doing here? Where did I come from? It's like some ghastly nightmare. I keep hoping I'm going to wake up—but I don't. It just keeps on going!'

'No one's even heard of you, Tee,' he interrupted roughly. 'Half of the Pacific has been talking about you all day—police from Christchurch to Hong Kong, coastguards, newspapers, radio, every rescue service you can think of and a lot more besides—nothing, Tee. No one's even reported a red catamaran missing. You might have dropped out of space on to that bare piece of rock. Or been born out of the sea-foam, like Aphrodite. But you're real.' He reached out and shook her shoulder hard. 'Do you hear me? You're damn well *real*. And that means you're going to have to work out your problem somehow. Which you won't do by blubbering on about being in a nightmare.'

She stared at him with wide green eyes, then slowly relaxed.

'Yes,' she said at last, her voice calm, 'you're right. Thank you for that, Mr Kavanagh. I needed it.'

'My name's Brendan,' he said. And for once the grey eyes were almost friendly.

'I hate being called Tee,' she said, dropping her eyes shyly.

'Beggars can't be choosers,' he said, amused.

'But it's—it's so impersonal. It makes me feel like—I don't know, like a *thing*, not a person.'

'Have you got any suggestions?' he enquired. 'Tilly? Topsy? Tabasco?'

'Please don't patronise me,' she said sharply.

'I see you're recovering,' he said, a dry glint in his eyes. 'Would you like to be called Thursday? That begins with a T—and I found you on a Thursday.'

'I'm not a stray dog,' she said bitterly. 'Thursday isn't a person's name.'

'Well,' he said, noting the flush that had spread through the satiny skin of her throat and cheeks, 'don't lose your temper. It doesn't really matter what I call you, anyway.' He stood up. 'I have to get *Seaspray* ready tonight. I'm sailing with the tide tomorrow.'

The flush faded, leaving her face pearly white, the pink blotches of sunburn standing out lividly.

'Leaving?' she whispered. 'Where to?'

'San Francisco,' he said casually. Her heart began to thud.

'In America? *America*? B-but you *can't*!'

'Why not?'

'You can't leave me here,' she said desperately. 'I'll go mad if you do. I don't know a single soul here—I don't even know who I am——'

'It'll all come back to you,' he said impatiently. 'Look, I must go——'

'It may not,' she said, trembling.

'What?'

'The psychiatrist told me this afternoon. He said there was a chance my memory might never return.' She began to sob quietly. 'Please don't leave me here——'

'I must,' he said, plainly disturbed, by her tears. 'For God's sake don't take on like that. I've got to deliver *Seaspray* to her new owner in San Francisco. And I have to pick up another boat there——'

'I'll die if you leave me,' she wailed, 'I'll die! I'll be utterly lost——'

'Oh, nonsense,' he said, coming back to her bedside. 'Listen—I'll be coming through these islands again in about a month or six weeks. And I'll come and see you then, I promise.'

'Six weeks?' She stared at him through tear-filled green eyes. 'In six weeks I could be anywhere. They want to put me in a lunatic asylum!'

'I'm sure that's not so,' he said quietly.

'They do,' she sobbed. 'I heard the psychiatrist say so to the doctor. He wants to fly me to Melbourne, and put me in a mental hospital there. He says they're going to if I don't get my memory back in two days!'

For the first time, pity touched the deep grey eyes.

'I'm sorry, Thursday,' he said gently. 'Maybe they'll be able to help you there. After all, they know all about the human mind——'

'*I am not mad!*' she told him fiercely, her blonde hair

falling over her eyes and clinging to the stickiness of her burned cheeks. 'And I'm not going to any madhouse!'

'Thursday——'

'If you go tomorrow,' she told him, her face a mask of desperation, 'I'll kill myself!'

'Don't be absurd——'

'And I'll tell them you raped me,' she pursued, her voice shaking. 'I'll say you attacked me, and that was why I lost my memory!'

He stared at her, his face set. She saw the big shoulders tense with anger.

'You can tell them what you damn well please,' he said icily. 'Do you think they'll believe you?'

'It'll stop you from leaving, at any rate,' she quavered. 'You'll have to stay here for days while they check you out. You won't get to San Francisco on time.'

'You little brat!' He stared at her in barely-suppressed fury. She glared back at him, hating herself for what she was doing. But she *couldn't* lose him. He was the only thing in the world that was real to her; the only person who knew that her story was true. Without him, she would be completely adrift.

And he might be the only key to her lost past.

'Please stay,' she begged. 'Just for another day.'

'I'm beginning to think you belong in a mental hospital,' he said through gritted teeth. 'I've already wasted precious days over you, saving your wretched life. And this is the thanks you give me!'

'All right,' she said, struggling angrily upright, 'You saved my life, Brendan. If you hadn't picked me off that rock, I would have died. Well, I'm still marooned—and if you don't pick me up again, I'm just going to die here.'

'That's immature rubbish,' he snapped.

'It's not,' she said, equally angrily. 'You just want to

think so. But having saved me, you're responsible for
me——'

'*Responsible* for you?' The grey eyes blazed. 'Who the
hell gave you that idea? No one's responsible for
anyone in this life, Thursday. It's a rotten world, and
it's each one for himself—and the sooner you learn
that, the better.'

She stared at him in misery. 'All right,' she said dully,
'then you're not responsible for me. But I'm going to
make sure you stay in Fiji—at least for another day—
for my own sake. After all,' she added bitterly, 'it's
everyone for himself, isn't it?'

'Damn you!' he grated, turning on his heel.

'Promise me you'll stay,' she pleaded. But he strode
out without replying, and she watched his broad,
straight back with mingled hope and despair.

She would be lucky if he stayed, she knew that. Yet
what she had said to him was true; if he was simply
going to abandon her here in this strange land,
friendless and lost, then he might as well have left her to
die in peace on Hunter Island, unknown and
unmourned.

CHAPTER TWO

She awoke the next morning with the tantalising feeling that she had dreamed about her past life during the night, but was unable to recall anything tangible. She had a feeling she could recall a big house—a big house filled with beautiful furniture. Did that mean she was rich? The daughter of a wealthy man? She had certainly dreamed about Brendan Kavanagh, because the smiling nurse who brought her breakfast in told her that she had called his name out several times.

'Seems like you got a little romance in your heart for that man,' the Fijian nurse had said teasingly.

She had tried to explain, then had given up. How could anyone understand?

After breakfast, they had shown her how the ugly raw patches on her body were beginning to heal. Even the bruises were beginning to fade, and her young body was slowly filling out after what had presumably been days of near-starvation. With a sudden shock, she realised that once these outwards signs of her ordeal were gone, there would be no evidence to account for her origins at all. Nothing except Brendan Kavanagh's testimony. And where was he? Had he already sailed for America, lost to her for ever among the dancing waves? The thought sent a chill through her, and she thrust it away.

She lay still, watching the tropical morning brighten through her window. Somehow, she knew she was English. This Pacific world was strange to her, utterly strange. How had she come here? And from where in England had she started? The doctor had left her with a battered old school atlas, and she had pored over the map of the British Isles, desperately hoping for a clue, a distant bell of memory. The names were all familiar. When she covered the counties with her hand, she could reel off the names of the principal cities and rivers without thinking. From this oddly-shaped island with its green and brown blotches, she must have come—travelling the thousands of miles to the South Pacific, and a rendezvous with destiny. But how? On holiday? On a business trip? And none of the names on the map struck any bells in her mind. She knew them all, and she could remember some of the principal buildings in the towns, even remember what they looked like.

Yet it was dead knowledge. Like the stuff you learned in school, a collection of names and figures and facts that you knew were true, without ever having actually experienced them. There was no mental image to accompany the information, no intimate personal recollection. She did not even have a name.

'Thursday,' she whispered to herself. What an ugly name it was, crudely unimaginative. The sort of name a Victorian beadle might have given to a foundling baby discovered on some doorstep. Thursday. Fourth day of the week. Named after Thor, the Scandinavian god of thunder. The day on which a stranger had picked her limp body off a barren rock in the middle of a vast ocean, God knows how many thousand miles from home. Thursday. That was all she had, the casual name a stranger had bestowed on her, as callously as though she had been a stray cat found starving in an alley.

She thought of Brendan Kavanagh's cool grey eyes. He was an unmistakably powerful, male presence—hard and efficient. There was a vigorous, ruthless energy in all his movements; she could play them back to herself on the screen of her mind—no other clutter was present to distract her. She could see the passionate curve of his mouth, the lithe, strong movements of his hands and shoulders, the hard, challenging glint of his sea-grey eyes. Only once had she seen those eyes clouded with compassion; to him, she was simply an obstacle in his way, to be kicked aside as quickly as possible.

She stirred restlessly. How on earth was she going to keep him with her? He had some appointment to keep in San Francisco. She had checked the distance in the atlas. Over five thousand miles from Fiji. An eternity of time and space. She couldn't let him go—she *couldn't*. Or if he went, then she must go with him. There were no other alternatives.

Her reverie was interrupted by the arrival of the senior charge nurse, a formidable Fijian matron of around sixty.

'I've got to have some name to put on these forms,' she said irritably, waving a sheaf of papers at her. 'You can't just be listed as an unknown white girl. And who is going to pay for your treatment, might I ask?'

'I don't know,' she faltered. She seemed to be saying that sentence a lot lately. It had become a sort of refrain.

'You don't know much, do you?' asked the matron caustically, as if reading her thoughts. 'Well, give me some name to put down—anything. Just choose a name.'

'Thursday,' she said without thinking. The nurse's eyebrows rose, but she bit back the sour comment that had obviously risen to her lips. 'Is that your first name?' she enquired, writing it down.

'Yes,' she nodded.

'Second name?'

She racked her brains feverishly. All she could come

up with was the name of the island where she had been found.

'Hunter,' she said. 'Thursday Hunter.'

'All right, Miss Thursday Hunter,' said the nurse, rising with a not unsympathetic nod, 'the psychiatrist will be on the ward in a few minutes.'

'Please,' Thursday said, as the nurse turned to go.

'Yes?'

'The man who brought me here—his name is Brendan Kavanagh. Please could you find out if he's still on the island for me?'

'I'll try,' said the nurse, writing the name down. 'Where is he staying?'

'I think he'll be on a yacht called *Seaspray*,' she said.

The nurse's eyebrows rose again. 'I'll do my best,' she said shortly. As she left, she bumped into the psychiatrist coming in.

The psychiatrist, a tall, mild-looking man in his late thirties, came over to her bedside with a smile.

'Good morning, young woman. Feeling any better?'

'Much better, thanks,' she smiled back.

'Any luck with the memory?'

'Well, I had some dreams last night——' She told him what she could recall about the big house, ending with an apologetic, 'It's not much, I'm afraid.'

'On the contrary, it's good progress,' he beamed. 'Very good indeed. What you dreamed of is very probably your own home back in England.'

'I only wish I could bring it back more clearly,' she said in frustration.

'Well,' he said, opening his briefcase with a businesslike air, 'I may have just the thing here.'

'What is it?' she asked apprehensively as he selected a little bottle and began to unwrap a disposable syringe.

'It's scopolamine,' he told her. 'It's a hypnotic drug used as an anaesthetic in most hospitals. If I give you a smallish injection of it, with a stimulant to keep you awake, it may help you to unlock your memory.'

She watched him fearfully as he squirted a thin stream of the liquid through his syringe and laid it on a kidney-basin.

'We'll just wait until Dr Taveuni gets here,' he said. 'Don't look so alarmed—it's not going to hurt.'

'I'm not afraid of the injection,' she said. 'I don't like the idea of being given all these drugs, that's all.'

He shook his head with a superior smile as he began filling a second syringe. 'This is quite standard practice,' he assured her. 'It may just work the trick.'

'And if it doesn't?'

'If it doesn't,' he said cheerfully, 'we'll send you to see some specialists in Melbourne.'

'You mean a madhouse,' she said tautly.

'Of course I don't,' he said, glancing at her sharply over the rims of his glasses. 'No one wants to lock you away, young lady. But they'll need to observe you for a few days or weeks before they know how to help you.'

'Observe me? Help me?' She glared at him with mutinous green eyes. 'I'm not a wild animal, Doctor! Nor am I insane——'

'No one said you were, young lady. I just——'

'My name is Thursday Hunter,' she said.

'You mean you've remembered it?' he asked in surprise.

'No,' she said. 'But I can't keep being called "young lady", or "the patient" all my life. Can I?'

'Thursday is a rather eccentric name,' he said drily, laying the second syringe next to the first.

'It's the day I was found on,' she explained, eyeing the syringes with a hostile air. 'I don't think I want to go through with this, Doctor.'

'Nobody's forcing you,' he reminded her.

The little Fijian doctor bustled in with a nurse in tow.
'Ah—Dr Adams,' he beamed. 'Shall we proceed?'

'Our patient—that is to say, Miss Hunter, is having
second thoughts, Dr Taveuni.' The psychiatrist smiled
with unexpected friendliness at Thursday. 'Listen, Miss
Hunter,' he told her gently, 'if you don't want these
injections, of course I won't give them to you. But they
represent one of the few chances you've got of
stimulating your memory by medical means. It may not
succeed. It's not even likely to,' he admitted calmly.
'But if you don't take this chance, you'll simply have to
wait until your mind decides to release its past
voluntarily.'

'Last night you said that might never happen,' she
said quietly.

He nodded. 'In some cases of amnesia, the memory
never returns. Usually, though, in those cases the
thalamus itself—the organ in the brain dealing with
recollection—has been damaged in some way.'

'And mine isn't?'

'There's no reason why it should be,' he smiled. 'In your
case, I'd say that the loss of memory was the result of a
prolonged psychological shock—your ordeal on the
island.' He sighed. 'The human mind is a great mystery,
my dear. Presumably it simply switched itself off in your
case, as a way to protect itself from further suffering. It
may switch itself on again at any time. In a few days,
perhaps. Memory often returns within a few days of being
lost. But it could take weeks—or years. It might not come
back at all, or not come back fully.' He exchanged glances
with the little Fijian doctor. 'My colleague and I don't
know much about amnesia,' he confessed with a wry
smile. 'I doubt whether anyone does.'

'Wouldn't it come back automatically if I saw
something I remembered? Or met someone I knew?' she
asked.

'Maybe,' he shrugged. 'There have been cases of amnesiacs not recognising their own husbands or wives, not remembering their own houses or families.'

'Oh, God!' she whispered fearfully.

'There is another aspect of it,' said the Fijian doctor unexpectedly. His face, like his voice, was homely and sympathetic. 'You've been deprived of your memory, something which to most people is a source of great pleasure and comfort. But that's not true of all people. Your memories, for example,' he smiled, 'may have been of suffering, or pain, or boredom. Dr Adams will confirm, I think,' he added, 'that something unpleasant in your memory may have contributed to your amnesia in the first place. You may not be missing all that much.'

'But I've lost my identity,' she said miserably. 'I don't know who I am!'

'That's a great exaggeration,' grinned the Fijian doctor. 'You're a very definite personality, believe me.' The other doctor and the nurse smiled. 'You are what you are,' he went on kindly. 'All you've lost is a very small parcel of tags or labels—name, age, address. Those can be replaced, Miss Hunter. Like all labels. You can't be more than twenty-one or two. To be absolutely frank, you didn't have a very big past to lose.'

'That's easy to say,' she said bitterly.

'True,' he admitted. 'But you're turning out very attractive indeed. All this burn-tissue,' he said, pointing to her face and shoulders, 'will be healed soon. With that blonde hair and those green eyes, you're going to be something of a stunner. If I'm any judge, that is. You'll be able to make a new life for yourself very soon. Much sooner than you expect. And when the old one returns—if it returns—you'll be able to just join it on.'

She lay in silence, digesting what they had said.

'Shall I try the scopolamine?' prompted the psychiatrist gently.

'Yes,' she sighed at last. 'Go ahead.'

The nurse dabbed her arm with a cool swab of alcohol, and the needle slipped under the skin. Thursday Hunter lay back on her pillows with a sigh. A kind of twilight settled gradually over her thoughts, and she relaxed completely.

'How are you feeling?' asked the doctor, his voice coming from many miles away.

'Peaceful,' she answered. Her mouth was dry, but otherwise she felt utterly at rest. She was just beginning to nod off to sleep when another needle pricked her arm.

'Don't worry—that's just to keep you awake,' said someone, she didn't quite know who. She floated in a cloudy land of dreams and whispers, her eyes shut. She could see the ocean, limitless and peaceful, extending for miles around her. She was floating just above the waves, drifting like a gull.

'Can you hear me?' asked a friendly voice. She nodded slowly. 'Good,' said the voice. 'What's your name?'

'I'm a gull,' she said peacefully.

'And a very beautiful gull,' said the voice, unperturbed by the nonsense. She knew she wasn't a gull, of course. What she had meant to say was that she *felt* like a gull. But surely, if one felt like a gull, then one really was a gull. Or not?

'Tell me your name, Gull,' said the voice.

'Thursday,' she sighed. 'My name is Thursday Hunter . . .'

'Is that your real name?' persisted the voice. She opened her eyes slowly. The window seemed unusually huge and bright, and she could see coconut palms and infinitely soft blue skies beyond.

'I don't know my real name,' she whispered. 'Brendan calls me Thursday.'

'Where were you born, then, Thursday?'

She thought hard, as hard as she could. The answer came swimming up through the drifting sea.

'I was born on Hunter Island,' she said . . .

She awoke, feeling headachy and irritable, in the middle of the afternoon. Her mouth was dry and tasted papery, and the restful feeling induced by the drug had worn off completely. She sat up in some confusion, and an instant nausea clutched at her, making her gag.

'Here.' Someone thrust a papier-maché basin under her nose, and she coughed wretchedly into it.

'Oh God,' she groaned, 'I could never become a drug addict!' She retched again, feeling as though her stomach was tearing loose from its moorings.

'I'm getting quite used to seeing you vomit,' said a deep voice resignedly. She blinked stupidly up at Brendan, suddenly aware that she probably didn't look her best with strands of saliva clinging to her chin. She fought the nausea down grimly, and wiped her face hastily on the flannel they had left for her.

'Female vanity,' he sighed. 'Go ahead and be sick properly—*I* don't care what you look like.'

'I'm quite all right, thank you,' she said shortly.

He shot her an ironic glance. Today he was wearing a loose South Sea Island shirt that set his mahogany-tanned skin off well. Crisp black hair, tinted with copper, was just visible against the velvety skin of his chest in the vee of the white collar.

'They didn't get very much out of you,' he told her. 'You seemed to be convinced you were some kind of seagull, according to the psychiatrist. But you didn't recall a single useful detail of your past life.'

'Oh.' Cold disappointment washed over her. Then she

looked up at him with sad green eyes. 'Thank you for staying, Brendan. It means a lot to me.'

'I didn't have much choice,' he retorted. 'Not when you blackmailed me so cleverly. Are you sure you weren't a gangster's moll in your former life?'

But there was a glint of wry humour in his deep grey eyes as he stared down at her, his fists on his slim hips. For all his size, he was as gracefully poised as a dancer or a bullfighter. The power of those broad, hard shoulders tapered down to a supple waist and taut, lithe hips that moved with poise and grace. His movements, she admitted unwillingly, were exciting—he carried his power with a grace that reminded her somehow of a proud ship in full sail, or a big stallion. She looked away shyly.

'I didn't want to blackmail you,' she muttered. 'And I could never have accused you, anyway.'

He arched an eyebrow.

'You know I would never have said—that—about you,' she said. 'Not after you'd saved my life.'

'Really?' he asked sceptically. He leaned forward. 'Listen, Thursday, we've just been having a big conference about you—the doctors and the Inspector and me. According to the head-shrinker, you refuse to go to this institution in Melbourne?'

'Wouldn't you?' she asked, shooting him a quick glance.

'It's your decision,' he shrugged. 'But there's nothing more this hospital can do for you, girl. They want to discharge you tomorrow.'

'Tomorrow?' she gasped. 'But—but——'

'This is only a small hospital, Thursday. And right now there's an Asian 'flu epidemic sweeping these islands. They need every bed they can get. You're just keeping some Fijian from the hospital treatment he needs by staying here. The sunburn will heal now, and there's literally no more medicine they can give you.'

She looked at him in horror. 'But what's going to happen to me?'

He sighed, his beautiful grey eyes troubled. 'You're in a bit of a mess, Thursday. You don't have a passport. You don't have a country of origin. By your looks and accent, you're very likely British. But you can't prove it, can you?'

She shook her head miserably.

'And the Inspector doesn't seem very keen on your staying here, either. Which boils down to one of two choices. Either you fly back to London—the British Consul here might just arrange your fare—and take your chance with the British Home Office. Or go to Australia, and apply for Australian citizenship. The Australians are quite willing to have you, providing you go through the official channels.'

'Which are?'

'Well, you'll need a medical check-up, for one thing. Some details of education, training, job experience——'

'But I don't *know* any of that stuff,' she said angrily. 'I could have a degree in nuclear physics for all I know! Besides, I don't want to go to Australia—I've never been there. I don't know anybody there.'

He shrugged again. 'They're very friendly, kind people,' he said. 'But if you don't like that idea, then go back to Britain.'

'I don't know anyone there, either,' she groaned. 'What am I going to do?'

'Well, you're going to have to decide,' he told her indifferently. 'And I'm leaving for America at midnight.' He held up a hand to silence her agonised protests. 'I'm sorry, Thursday, but I can't wait any longer. Don't try and stop me. Not this time.'

She was about to plead with him when the little Fijian doctor bustled in.

'Ah, the little seagull is awake. How are you feeling, Miss Hunter?'

'Sick,' she said. 'Are you really going to discharge me tomorrow?'

'We don't have much choice,' he told her calmly. 'We have a huge waiting-list of patients, and we need every available bed. There's an epidemic at the moment, I'm afraid—it usually turns up about this time of year.' He smiled at her. 'You're a fit, healthy young woman. All you need is some good feeding, and to take care of those burns.' He glanced at Brendan. 'Has Mr Kavanagh explained what options are open to you?'

'Such as they are,' she said bitterly.

'Until either you regain your memory, or someone turns up to account for you, I'm afraid those are the only options you have,' said the doctor quietly. 'If you want my advice, Miss Hunter, I'd go and see the British Consul in Brisbane and ask him to arrange for you to return to the United Kingdom.'

'Where in the United Kingdom?' she asked angrily. 'Aberdeen? Bangor? Stockton-on-Tees?'

'Why not try London?'

'London? And who do I see in London? How am I to support myself? Where am I to stay?'

'You've got a tendency to whine,' Brendan Kavanagh said mildly. 'If you'll stop feeling so damned sorry for yourself for five minutes, you might get somewhere.'

She shot him an angry glance, meeting those damnable grey eyes.

'It's easy for the strong to criticise the weak,' she retorted.

His full lower lip curled angrily. 'You're not weak,' he told her, 'just self-pitying.'

'Well, you're well out of it, aren't you?' she snapped bitterly. 'You're getting on your boat and sailing away.

It's very easy for you to tell me to stop feeling sorry for myself—it's not your life!' Her eyes were bright with angry tears. 'God! I wish you'd left me to die on Hunter Island.'

'Perhaps I should have done,' he said, his passionate mouth curling into a contemptuous curve. 'But don't think I'm running away from you, Thursday. You simply don't mean that much to me. I've got a boat to deliver in San Francisco, and I'm damn well going to deliver it.'

'Take me with you,' she said impulsively.

'What?' He stared for a second, then burst into laughter. 'Please—no more craziness, Thursday. I've got——'

'You found me,' she said urgently. 'You brought me into this world—you at least owe me that.'

'I've already told you,' he said grimly, 'I don't owe you a damn thing, girl. Now, let's not even think about this ridiculous notion any longer.'

The Fijian doctor, who had been looking thoughtfully from Thursday to Brendan, interposed.

'How long will your voyage take, Mr Kavanagh?'

'About a month,' he shrugged.

'And I presume you're coming back again?'

'Yes.' He looked at the doctor with hostile sea-grey eyes. 'If you've got any ideas about my taking Thursday with me, doctor——'

'How are you coming back?' asked the little Fijian with a disarming smile.

'I'm picking up a schooner yacht in San Francisco,' he said. 'I'll be sailing her back along the same route. Which is why I've told Thursday that I'll come and see her on my way back to Sydney next month.'

'Big deal,' she said in a low voice. But she looked at the doctor with dawning hope.

'Tell me,' pursued the doctor with a cunning glint in

his eye, 'these long solo voyages—they're very lonely, aren't they?'

'Dr Taveuni,' he replied drily, 'I can see right through you. I don't want this girl on board, and that's flat.'

'Why not?' demanded Thursday. 'I'll be able to cook, at least——'

'If you can remember how to break an egg,' he said sarcastically.

'You know, Mr Kavanagh, I'm inclined to agree with Miss Hunter.' The doctor smiled gently at Thursday. 'Once you save a life, you are responsible for it.'

'Is that a Fijian proverb?' retorted Brendan.

'As a matter of fact it is,' said the little doctor with a smile. 'On Fiji, the saving of a life—especially at sea—has a great significance. In the old days, for example, if someone whose life you had saved went on to commit a murder, then you were liable for the crime.' He nodded sagely. 'It's true. On Fiji, if you save a life, then they say you are responsible for that life for ever afterwards.'

'That seems rather hard on the life-saving party,' Brendan growled.

'It was a law which had a lot of very good points about it,' said the Fijian. 'Of course, the debt could be cancelled—if the other person managed in his turn to save your life.'

'I appreciate the lecture in Fijian social anthropology,' Brendan nodded austerely. 'But it's not getting us anywhere. And you, Dr Taveuni,' he added, pointing at the little man, 'have a reputation among these islands for being able to talk the hind leg off a donkey—and for being able to charm the birds out of the trees.'

'Maybe so,' grinned Dr Taveuni. 'But you've also got a reputation among these islands—as a man of scrupulous integrity. A hard man, true; but a man who would always stop to help a fellow human being in trouble. And

Thursday happens to be in trouble right now—you have it in your power to do the one thing that might give her a chance to regain her memory. Which I don't think she'll ever do being badgered in hospitals.'

'I'm not a charitable foundation, Taveuni—I've got my own affairs to run!'

'But I wouldn't get in your way!' Thursday promised in anguish. 'I could be a real help to you!'

'I don't see where this discussion is getting us,' Brendan said dismissively. 'Why should I take this girl along with me?'

'I am not "this girl",' she said fiercely. 'I've got a name now. And what Dr Taveuni said made a lot of sense to me.'

'It would do,' he retorted, his beautiful eyes scornful.

'Why should you take her along?' The doctor paused. 'Because you are the only person in the world she knows. Because you saved her life. Because going with you on this journey may give her the rest she needs to recover her memory.'

'And what if she remembers that she's a mass murderer?' he protested.

'Don't be so hard on her,' said the doctor, hushing the retort that had sprung to Thursday's lips. 'She doesn't look like a mass murderer to me. You know, when she was under the scopolamine that Dr Adams injected her with, you were the only thing she talked about? From first to last, all she talked about was Brendan Kavanagh. For a lot of the time,' he added, smiling quietly at Thursday, 'she seemed to imagine that you were actually in the room—and she talked to you non-stop.'

'So what?' retorted Brendan. But he looked rather gentler.

'So—she responds to you. If anyone can help her recover her memory, Mr Kavanagh, you can.'

'Your Fijian logic is a trifle bewildering,' he said drily. 'I'm no psychiatrist, Dr Taveuni. There's nothing I can do for Thursday Hunter.'

'I don't think she needs a psychiatrist,' the doctor replied. 'What she needs is companionship, rest, good food. She could be very useful to you—as she says, she could cook, help you with sailing, look after things while you slept, or if you got ill. And if after all she doesn't remember anything more about her past, you can simply drop her off here—or in Australia—on your way back.'

'You make it sound so easy,' Brendan said. The cloudy grey eyes were thinking hard. Trembling inside, Thursday waited for his verdict.

'No,' he said suddenly, shaking his head. 'The thing's impossible. For one thing, she doesn't even have a passport. The Americans wouldn't allow her to step off the boat.'

'They would give her a temporary entry permit on the understanding that she was leaving again within a specified period, though,' said the doctor.

'You're in the wrong profession,' said Brendan, half admiringly, half angrily. 'You should have been a defence lawyer, Dr Taveuni.'

'But he's right,' Thursday interposed urgently. 'And I could be a help to you—I swear it! After all, I was on a catamaran, wasn't I? That proves I must have known something about sailing, doesn't it?'

'I thought you'd lost your memory,' he said with quiet irony.

'I have—but I could still ride a bicycle. I'm sure you can't forget things like that.' She looked to the doctor for confirmation. 'Can you? And I'm quite strong, really—I could pull ropes or weigh anchors or whatever——'

'I'm sorry,' Brendan interrupted regretfully. 'It just

can't be done, Thursday. I don't have the time to wait around for you. I'm sailing on the midnight tide, and that's flat.'

'You won't have to wait,' she said with growing excitement. 'After all, I don't have any bags to pack or anything. I'll be with you by midnight!'

'That's crazy,' he smiled. 'You're not even well enough.'

'I am! I'm fine!' She turned to the doctor with pleading green eyes. 'Tell him I'm fit.'

'She is still weak, of course,' said the doctor gently, 'and she'll have to take care of herself. But there's no reason why she shouldn't join you tonight.'

'In what?' he demanded. 'In that blue negligee? You can't set out on a six- or seven-week voyage with no clothes. You'll need anoraks, seaboots, jerseys, warm clothes of every kind. You don't have any seagoing gear at all.'

She slumped back in despair. 'I hadn't thought of that,' she said, close to tears. 'I don't even have the money to pay for my hospital treatment.'

'I don't think the Fijian government will mind paying for that,' Taveuni said gently. He surveyed Thursday's tragic face with friendly brown eyes, then looked up at Brendan.

'About how much would it cost to equip her for the trip to America and back?' he enquired softly.

'I'm beginning to think you're both crazy,' Brendan sighed. 'It would cost hundreds. And before you think of lending her the money,' he added holding up a hand to silence the little doctor, 'just remember that it's four-thirty now. And I'm sailing at midnight exactly. By the time you get her dressed and out of here, every shop in Lautoka will be closed.'

The glimmer of hope in Thursday's eyes faded. The Fijian doctor shook his head slightly.

'The position isn't all that bad,' he murmured. 'My brother-in-law runs the marine supplies store behind the pier. He ought to have everything we need. And I'm sure he'll stay open after hours for us.'

'You—you mean you'd lend me the money?' Thursday gasped, joy beginning to shine in her face.

'I trust you to pay me back some day,' the little man nodded with a smile.

Brendan's eyes were cold.

'Doctor,' he said quietly, 'tell me one thing—what makes you so damned keen that Thursday Hunter should come with me on *Seaspray*?'

'You could call it an instinct, I suppose,' he replied with a smile. 'There are no miracle cures for amnesia, Mr Kavanagh—there's not a psychiatrist living who could help Thursday Hunter right now. Yet you might be able to do for her what no doctor could—give her the chance to find herself again. Give her the time, the moral support, the patience, to open the locked doors inside her mind.'

The grey eyes met hers, then flicked back to the doctor.

'Are you trying to tell me that this woman's recovery depends on me?' he asked bluntly.

'Maybe it does,' the doctor nodded. 'On you and on *Seaspray*. The sea took her memory. Maybe the sea will give it back again.'

'Your Fijian proverbs are very poetic, Dr Taveuni,' Brendan snorted.

'Mr Kavanagh—Brendan—I'm asking you not only as a Fijian, but as a medical man; please take Thursday with you. She needs you—and no one else here has the time or the ability to fulfil her need. Please don't refuse her.'

There was a quiet pause. Brendan turned to her, his face expressionless.

'And you? What do *you* think of all this medical mumbo-jumbo, Thursday Hunter?'

'I want to go with you,' she whispered, hope striving against despair inside her. 'I don't know if the doctor's right or not. All I know is that I can't stay here without you.'

'This is pure blackmail,' he said grimly, rubbing his cheek hard. The grey eyes thought hard for long seconds, then he nodded curtly.

It was as simple as that.

'Let me make one thing perfectly clear at the outset,' he said softly. 'If you come with me on *Seaspray*—for whatever reason—we're going to do things my way. You may not like it, but I'm captain of *Seaspray*, Thursday. What I say goes. There's only room for one commander on an ocean-going yacht. Is that understood?'

'Yes,' she said breathlessly, her heart pounding.

'Then let's get going.'

She looked up at the smiling doctor with sparkling green eyes, too happy to speak.

'I have a feeling,' the doctor said happily, 'that you two are going to be very good for one another.'

'It isn't a wedding,' Brendan commented sourly. 'Can you get her some clothes?'

'Certainly,' he agreed promptly, and called into the corridor. 'Nurse! I'm going to discharge Miss Hunter right away. Can you rustle up some clothes for her? A nurse's uniform would do.'

'Yes, doctor,' said the nurse, peering into the ward with an astonished face, 'whatever you say!'

CHAPTER THREE

Tom Kandavu, the little doctor's burly brother-in-law, heaved the last bag into place under Thursday's bunk.

'You can unpack it all and stow it properly tomorrow,' he said, then took her hand in both of his great paws.

'Have a nice trip, Miss Hunter. And I sure hope you get your memory back soon.'

'I don't know how to thank you,' she said, close to tears. 'You've been so very kind to me——'

'It's been my pleasure, my pleasure,' Kandavu assured her with a beaming smile. He bustled out of the little cabin, past the doctor. 'Goodnight, Paul—see you Sunday.'

'See you, Tom. And thanks.'

'No sweat, brother!'

Dr Taveuni turned to Thursday with a happy expression on his homely face.

'So,' he smiled, 'things move quickly in Fiji, eh?' She laughed rather tremulously. 'I've packed a course of vitamin tablets in your dunnage,' he said more seriously. 'You'll find them in the big plastic tub. You probably don't need them—but take them all the same.' They looked at one another by the light of the small oil-lamp that swayed gently against the bulkhead. 'So long, Thursday Hunter,' Paul Taveuni said gently. 'See you in two months' time.'

She opened her mouth to say something, then shook her head. 'You've been very good to me,' she said in a low whisper. 'Thank you, doctor.'

44

'As my brother-in-law says, no sweat.' He took her shoulders in his little hands and kissed her with fatherly affection on the cheek. 'This voyage may not be in keeping with the best medical traditions,' he smiled, 'and I might tell you that Dr Adams still doesn't have any idea that you're leaving. But I feel in my heart of hearts that this is the right thing for you to do.'

She nodded silently, her eyes shining.

'Also,' he added with a grin, 'it gets you out of *my* hair for six or seven weeks!' He checked his wristwatch. 'It's nearly ten o'clock. I'm going to get back to my family, and leave you to get ready for your departure. Good luck Thursday.' With a final shake of the hand, the Fijian turned to climb up the companionway. She followed him up on to the deck, where Brendan Kavanagh was adjusting the steering-vane in the stern of the yacht. He looked up, the Tilley lamp by which he was working carving silver patterns across his face and chest. He secured the vane with a tug of the line, and came over to help the Fijian doctor down the short gangplank. The two men shook hands as Thursday leaned against the fibreglass coaming of the cockpit, her eyes full of tears.

'Well, Dr Taveuni,' Brendan said with a half-smile, 'you seem to have wangled your patient on board my yacht. I still don't know how you did it.'

'Lood after her, Brendan,' the doctor grinned. 'I'll be seeing you in a few weeks.'

'With luck,' the other man muttered drily. 'Goodbye, Paul.'

'Goodbye. Goodbye, Thursday!'

They watched the small figure step into his battered old car and drive off cautiously along the decidedly rickety pier, his headlights picking out a path through the confusion of nets and upturned boats towards the town. As he rounded the last corner, they heard the impudent sound of his hooter coming across on the warm night breeze.

Brendan turned to her.

'Well,' he said calmly, 'you've managed to get your way, Thursday.'

'Don't be angry with me,' she said softly. 'I swear I won't get in your way.'

'I'm not angry with you,' he said drily. 'But I definitely will be if you *do* get in my way.' He stepped across the short afterdeck to the steering-vane. 'I'm having a little trouble with this,' he said as he squatted down to his task by the flaring white light of the lamp. 'I'll just get it rigged up, and then I'll show you one or two essentials before we set sail. After that,' he grunted, tightening a nut with a spanner, 'you and I will have to have a little talk.'

She stood by the wheel, watching his broad back as he went about his work with sure, elegant movements. The aluminium mast just behind her rose forty feet up into the velvety night sky. Sailless, it clinked musically as the breeze rapped a loose nylon guy-rope against it from time to time. A slightly shorter mast rose through the foredeck, just in front of the cockpit coaming. *Seaspray* was about thirty-six feet long, she judged, and even in the moonlight of the small harbour she could see that all her tackle and her winches were gleaming new, her decks spotless and bright with fresh varnish. Brendan ignored her completely as he worked. And for the first time, the reality of what was about to happen began to dawn on her. An electric thrill of mingled fear and excitement shot through her. It was only a very few days since she had first awoken—no, first come to life, been born almost, aboard this very boat. And now she was setting off on a journey of some six thousand miles, across an unknown ocean, to an unknown land.

Dear God! What was she doing? This was how Columbus must have felt on the brink of his voyage into the unknown. Paul Taveuni had been right: things *did* happen fast on Fiji. Well, she was certainly learning about herself. Was this the sort of person she was? The sort of impulsive, obstinate person who would leap out into the unknown void at the drop of a hat? There was the question, too, that she knew next to nothing about Brendan Kavanagh, the ruthless, handsome man with whom she was going to be sharing a very small world for the next weeks.

As they had selected gear and stores in Tom Kandavu's marine supplies shop, Paul Taveuni had told her that Brendan Kavanagh was a yachtsman who frequently passed through Fiji and the neighbouring islands, and who had a reputation for hard efficiency, utter dependability—and independence.

'In a sense,' the doctor had mused, 'I'm selling both of you a pig in a poke. I don't know Brendan Kavanagh that well, Thursday. I would trust him, on the strength of his reputation—but I don't know him as a friend. On the other hand,' he had smiled, 'I don't know you very well either. So it's a bit of an experiment, if the truth be known.'

Tom had snorted from behind a pile of brightly-coloured anoraks.

'You better hope they turn out good for each other, Paul. That Brendan Kavanagh looks as though he packs a mighty mean punch!'

'I'll remember to duck,' Dr Taveuni had smiled. 'But I feel it in my heart, Thursday, that this is the right thing to do. I can't explain it rationally—call it some kind of Island voodoo if you like—but I know this is going to turn out right for you.'

'It's better than going to a mental hospital,' she had agreed fiercely. 'Or getting tangled up in bureaucratic red tape for ever. I just wish Brendan were happier about it all.'

'He won't take too kindly to your presence at first,' the little doctor had warned her, trying oilskin hats on her blonde head for size, 'especially as we've bullied him into it. But he's scrupulously fair, and if you prove yourself—well, like I said, you'll become fast friends.'

'He's a mighty tough character in some ways,' the burly Tom Kandavu had put in. 'And he has a reputation with the ladies, too—so you watch out.'

'I don't think he's a ladies' man,' the doctor had contradicted quietly. 'He's undeniably attractive to women, though—and he's had plenty of Fijian hearts fluttering—but he's a good man.'

Thursday had been too excited really to listen. She had nodded, hauling sea-boots on, but hadn't really thought about what the two islanders were saying.

Now, in the warm tropical night, under a moon that was more than half-full, under a thick shower of diamond stars, the reality of her enterprise was at last sinking home. She felt like a fledgling bird, poised on the edge of the dark, waiting to fly. Where to? She couldn't say.

Brendan rose from the stern, picking up the mini-sun of the Tilley lamp, and stepped over the coaming into the cockpit.

'Come along, First Mate,' he said briskly, 'I want to show you how the radio works.'

'Aye-aye,' she smiled nervously.

The white sails were ghostly in the moonlight. The light breeze filled them out as soon as Brendan had winched them up the twin masts; and as he hauled the boom over to the right, the yacht slid forward through the rippling water. At once, the deck seemed to come alive under Thursday's booted feet. The gentle rocking motion of a yacht at her moorings had given way to an eager, thrusting surge of power. A deep thrill ran through her veins, and she clung to the little rail on top of the coaming in excitement.

Brendan stepped lightly into the cockpit, bumping her with his hard shoulder as he did so, and took the brass-rimmed wheel.

'There are two buoys at the harbour entrance—we're supposed to steer between them, but the tide tends to pull them away from their moorings.'

She looked back at the glimmering lights of Lautoka behind them. An almost frighteningly large expanse of glimmering water had come between them already, and the tiny lights were already beginning to fade. The warm smell of the land, slightly fragrant with frangipani blossom, lingered on the salt air. Then *Seaspray* began to pitch among an expanse of white water, almost throwing Thursday off her feet.

'We're passing through the harbour entrance,' he told her. 'It won't last long.'

And within minutes, the pitching had given way to a long, deep swell that rocked the surging boat smoothly and powerfully as she sliced through the dark water.

'Is that the ocean?' she asked breathlessly.

'The Pacific,' he nodded. 'We're still in fairly shallow water—but we'll be breasting rollers like this from now on.' He turned to look at her, his grey eyes questioning. 'All right?'

'I'm fine,' she smiled nervously.

'Good.' He switched off the Tilley lamp, and the night settled around them, illuminated only by the green glow of the instruments and the navigation lights up ahead. 'How about cocoa and a sandwich?' he commanded.

She nodded, though reluctant to leave the deck, and ducked down to the little galley just below.

As she made the snack, she could hear him moving around up on the deck, and when she climbed up again with her hands full, Brendan had hoisted a spinnaker. The big, full-bellied sail was hauling them along at what seemed to her a very respectable speed—though the darkness made it hard to judge.

'I keep hoping that some of this will strike me as familiar,' she said as they drank the sweet brew. 'If I'd managed to sail a catamaran single-handed—whatever a catamaran is—then I must have known something about sailing, mustn't I?'

'Presumably,' he shrugged. 'Though the cat was just a light fibreglass thing, not really suited for ocean sailing.' He shot her a glance in the warm darkness. 'As a matter of fact, that's one of the things I wanted to talk about,' he said. He threw the dregs of his cocoa over the side, and engaged the electric auto-pilot. 'Are you tired?'

'A little,' she confessed. 'But not if you want to talk.'

'I do,' he nodded. 'Let's sit here for a minute.' At the back of the cockpit was a sheltered seating area, protected by a spray hood and equipped with a row of comfortable seats. They sat down in the stillness of the night.

'I've been checking *Seaspray*'s log for the past fortnight,' he told her, 'trying to work out how the prevailing winds were blowing. And I've been trying to reconstruct what might have happened to you. Interested?'

'Very,' she nodded.

'I didn't pay too much attention to that catamaran on Hunter Island—it was pretty badly smashed up on the reef, and there was no way I could get to it. But it was a fairly small standard production model, from what I could see—they're made by the thousand in several countries, including Australia.'

She nodded her understanding.

'Right—so that gives us very little clue as to where you set out from. But if we assume that the most likely thing happened, we can make some kind of analysis. And the most likely thing that happened was that you—and maybe someone else set out from some place in the vicinity of Hunter, were caught up in a gale, blown a long way off your course, and ended up on the reefs at Hunter. Does that sound logical?'

'I suppose so,' she said slowly. 'But—you said there might have been someone else with me. What did you mean by that?'

'Someone who fell overboard and drowned,' he said indifferently.

'Oh, my God!'

'It's just a theory,' he shrugged, his handsome face impassive. 'But supposing the person who was with you—let's call him—or her—Charlie—supposing Charlie was the only person who knew who you were. The only person who came with you on a holiday, for example. Then Charlie's death effectively deprived you of your background. What I'm saying is that the only person who might know who you are may be lying at the bottom of the ocean—hey! Are you all right?'

She nodded weakly. 'Yes,' she whispered. 'I just felt faint for a second.' She laid her hand on her beating heart. 'That never occurred to me,' she breathed.

'Those catamarans can be sailed by either one or two people,' he said. 'Let's assume that you and Charlie were camping on a beach somewhere on the east coast of Australia. Or maybe in some private holiday cottage. No hotel registration, no details, nobody really knew you were there. Right?'

She nodded.

'Right. So, you and Charlie decide to go for a sail one afternoon. You get about a mile from the coast, when a big gale starts brewing up. You didn't bother to check the weather report, because you only intended to be out for a few hours. Are you following me?'

'Yes,' she whispered, frozen with horror and fascination.

'Well, the gale is a pretty big one, and you can't get back in. The wind blows you a good few miles out to sea within a few hours. You lose sight of the coast. And you don't have any compasses or foul weather gear. Pretty soon night falls. Driving rain, huge waves, frightening wind—you're both becoming exhausted and weak. Maybe you've got some emergency rations, maybe not. Anyhow, you're both clinging to the catamaran in this terrible weather. But in the night Charlie gets sleepy—or maybe the boom swings over and cracks his head open. Maybe even a passing shark takes a bite at——'

'*Stop!*' she gasped, covering her ears with her hands and squeezing her eyes shut against the image.

'In any case,' he continued imperturbably, 'something happens to Charlie—and when the dawn breaks, you're alone on the boat. Now, according to *Seaspray*'s log, there were force eight and nine winds blowing for almost ten days during the period you might have been at sea. Those are big winds, Thursday, enough to destroy most small craft. But also strong enough to drive you a thousand miles from Australia to Hunter Island. It's just possible.' His strong hand tilted her chin up so that he could look into her eyes. 'It's just possible, Thursday. And maybe thinking along those lines will strike a few chords in your mind.'

'Maybe,' she whispered.

'I broke the idea to you pretty roughly,' he acknowledged. 'But I wanted to try and shock you into stimulating that paralysed memory of yours.' He brushed her fair hair with a rough caress. 'And if you *had* lost someone close to you—a girl friend, say, or perhaps a lover—then the shock of that, and of finding yourself alone in a small boat in a gale, might have been enough to make you lose your memory.' He smiled slightly at her, his authoritative mouth almost friendly. 'I find it hard to believe that a girl as spirited as you could lose her memory simply through being adrift. No—there must be more to it than that.' He stood up and stretched his big shoulders. 'These psychiatrists tend to underestimate the power and resilience of the human mind,' he said drily. 'Are you okay, kid?'

'Just a bit stunned by your theory,' she admitted shakily.

He nodded. 'Just remember that it is a theory—nothing more. It could explain how you came to be in the vicinity of Hunter Island. My guess is that your sails must have been carried away towards the end of the storm. The current would have washed you on to Hunter—probably on that Monday or Tuesday. After the catamaran was wrecked, you may have managed to wade ashore—cutting your legs against the coral in the process. Once on the beach, you probably just collapsed. By the state of your sunburn, you'd been lying in the sun for about two days, perhaps in a coma. Definitely in a state of shock.' He strode over to the wheel to check the binnacle compass, then turned back to her. 'You weren't wearing very much when I found you. Just a very torn silk shirt, a pair of denim shorts, and a bikini bottom. And your famous chain,' he added, touching the silver thing at her throat with a finger. 'I just took your clothes off and threw them overboard—they were in a very bad state. It seems crazy now, but I didn't check them for name-tags before I chucked them out. It didn't occur to me that you would be suffering from amnesia. All I wanted to do was to wash the salt off you and clean your wounds.'

She nodded, grateful that the night was hiding the flush that had risen to her cheeks at the thought of this hard stranger undressing her unconscious body and touching her naked skin. As if sensing her embarrassment, he laughed shortly.

'Yours wasn't the first naked body I've seen, Thursday. And my thoughts were pure, I assure you.'

'I'm sure they were,' she said sarcastically.

'There's no need for embarrassment, girl,' he said with a touch of irritation. 'We're going to be seeing a lot of each other during this voyage. Literally. Besides,' he added with a characteristic shrug, 'you've got a beautiful body. It's nothing to be ashamed of.'

'It is now,' she said in a low voice. 'It's not beautiful any more.'

'Those burns will heal,' he said indifferently. 'You won't even be able to see them in a few weeks.'

'Do you believe that?' she asked quietly.

'Of course,' he said with a touch of impatience.

'One of the very first things I remember,' she told him in the same quiet voice, 'is waking up in that bunk down below and hearing you say that I could be scarred for life.'

There was a pause. 'For someone who's lost her memory, you certainly manage to remember everybody else's mistakes,' he said drily.

'I don't have anything else to remember,' she said with a slight smile.

'It's very late,' he said, checking his watch again. 'You'd best go below and get some sleep, Thursday. I'll stay on the bridge for the next few hours and catnap. Off you go.'

Nodding her thanks, she carried the mugs and plates down to the galley, rinsed them under the seawater tap, and went to her cabin to turn in. It was nearly one-thirty, and very dark down in the little cabin. She slid between the sheets, remembering how she had awoken in this very bunk on that dreadful morning, and curled up on her side. The tugging pain of her sunburned shoulders and breasts reminded her of her disfigurement, and she sighed. Deliberately, she made her mind relax. When she had first awoken in this cabin, her memory had been a blank sheet of paper. Now, only a week later, it was crammed with images—the hospital, the little Fijian doctor, the grey glint of Brendan Kavanagh's eyes, the pain of her burns.

Her burns. Were they ever going to heal? It had taken her a long time in the little hospital to accept that this was her body—this painful thing, covered with its ugly raw-pink blotches. Her honey-coloured skin was fine and satiny, and the savage heat of the tropical sun had torn at it cruelly. Across her cheeks and nose the skin had fallen away in strips, leaving her face like a child's crayon map. She was certain that the rawness would disappear in time; but would such delicate skin ever fully recover? Would it ever return to the silky softness it had once had?

There was little doubt that this sea-voyage was going to be beneficial. And not just because of the peace and quiet, either; there was something about Brendan's aggressive, sometimes abrasive presence that stimulated her, stirred her heart and mind. He was like a tonic. Maybe he was more.

Carefully she stopped her thoughts at that point. The last thing she wanted was to get emotionally confused about him. What she needed was rest.

Perhaps she would dream of that beautiful house again?

She lay quietly, allowing her mind to drift. Gradually, her body relaxed, and soon she was rocking gently in her bunk to *Seaspray*'s eager movements.

The green waves were gigantic, covered with racing foam. They towered over the little boat like demonic giants, smashing down at her with earth-shattering power. She clung to the cold mast desperately as the liquid-steel muscles of the water tried to tear her loose. Savage salt fingers clawed at her face, thrusting the bitter sea down her nose and throat, and she tried to scream, her lungs bursting. Above her, the scarlet Dacron sail battered and snapped in the gale, smashing the mast against her cheeks as she choked for air in this hell of whirling water.

The waves had faces, cruel, monstrous faces distorted by anger, that bellowed at her with gaping black mouths and then slid into a million demented shapes around her, reaching out slippery sinews to pull her down to destruction. But she did not give in. She clung to the aluminium mast with agonised, dogged strength as the hideous green faces swirled and snarled all around her. The boom was swinging loose, a long pole that occasionally battered at her shoulders, and then whirled round uselessly.

The red boat spun helplessly among the green and white mountains that stamped past remorselessly, savagely, determined to trample her into the icy depths. The crazy giants' faces bellowed down at her, cavernous mouths rimmed with flickering white teeth, monstrous gullets open to swallow her. She shut her eyes against the horror, burying her face against her aching arms.

And then, with a rending sound that rose above the fury of the storm, the red sail tore loose from the long grove in the mast. She stared in terror as the wind snatched it up with gigantic playfulness and whirled the red triangle across the waves like a scrap of plastic on an autumn day. The shrouds parted with a deep twang, and the mast shivered against her like a doomed creature. She had thought that fear had died in her heart many days ago. But now it had begun to pound in her again—the fear of death, the horror of drowning in this savage sea, of being dragged down into the icy depths by the murderous hands of the current, of drifting under the cold water, waiting for the scavenging teeth of some shark—

The sea drove a fist into her face, and she began to scream, choking on the bitter salt water that was thrusting its way into her lungs. The mast was torn loose from her grasp, and she felt herself slipping over the smooth wetness of the deck towards the hungry maw of the sea, which opened a gaping mouth to receive her. She screamed, again and again, trying to dig her fingernails into the unyielding surface of the fibreglass deck, slipping, falling—

The rock thumped into her chest with sudden force, and she clung to it desperately, clawing at its rough surface for a hold, clinging to it as she sobbed and choked. Someone was speaking in her ear, a deep voice that cut through the anger of the storm, a voice that soothed and gentled.

The spray faded around her in wraiths, and she found herself in his arms, clinging to him with aching hands. Sobs were still racking her as he cradled her gently, his arms strong and secure around her.

'It's all right, honey,' he murmured gently, 'it's not happening. Just a dream. You're all right.'

Slowly her sobs eased, and she lolled her head against his shoulder, tasting the salt of her own tears in her mouth. She had begun to shiver now, and she tried to fight back her crying.

'I'm s-sorry,' she whispered. 'I had a terrible nightmare. I d-dreamed I was drowning——'

'It's over now,' he said firmly, holding her close.

'But it was *real*,' she whispered. 'It was what happened to me—I know it!'

He laid her back down on the pillows and looked at her with deep grey eyes. The soft light of the oil-lamp gilded her skin, and she looked back at him with still frightened green eyes.

'Do you remember anything about it?' he asked.

'Everything,' she nodded with a shiver. 'The sea had faces—and the boat was red, like you said——' She clung to his arms. 'I know what a catamaran is now. It's a yacht with two hulls, isn't it?'

'Yes,' he nodded quietly.

'And I saw the sails being blown away. That was when I started screaming——'

'You don't remember anyone with you?' he asked, giving her a searching look.

'I was alone,' she said, shaking her head. 'There was no one else. But the sea——' She closed her eyes with a shudder, seeing the march of the great green waves in her mind. 'Dear Heaven, the sea!'

'Snap out of it,' he commanded roughly. She blinked at him, and he nodded. 'That's better. You've only been asleep for a few hours, Thursday. It's barely five-thirty—do you want to try and sleep some more?'

'I don't know,' she said shakily. 'Is the sun up?'

'It's just coming up now,' he told her.

She smiled at him tremulously. 'I think I'll go up on deck, then. Shall I bring you some coffee?'

'Good idea,' he nodded. She suddenly noticed that she was still clinging to his arms, and she relaxed her damp hands with an effort.

'Thank you for coming to my rescue,' she said quietly. 'I was about to drown when you woke me.'

'I couldn't exactly ignore you,' he said, his mouth curving into an ironic smile. 'You were screaming my name loud enough.'

'Was I?' she asked in some confusion.

'Don't you remember?' he asked drily. 'Yes, you were

howling for me like a lost soul. I thought the boat had sprung a leak, at the very least!'

She dropped her eyes, feeling unutterably stupid.

'I'm no authority on amnesia,' he said, 'but I would guess that dreams like this one are one of the ways you'll get your memory back. And you may get more of them over the next weeks.' He stood up, and opened the cabin door. 'I'll see you on deck,' he said, and climbed up the companionway into the cool dawn air. She pulled on jeans and a long-sleeved cotton shirt, and followed him up, pausing to make coffee in the galley.

The sun was a glowing orange oval just above the horizon as she came up, and the sea was calm, a glittering turquoise sheet streaked with swathes of silver where the wind had flattened the waves. The complete absence of land gave her a slight shock. The horizon was absolutely clean, a thin dark circle that extended around *Seaspray*, between the blue of the sky and the blue of the sea.

They sipped their coffee quietly, each preoccupied with their own thoughts, as the white yacht slid through the calm sea.

'This is what my mind feels like sometimes,' she said quietly, and Brendan lifted an enquiring eyebrow. She gestured at the horizon. 'Like an empty sea, bounded by a smooth horizon. At the moment it's calm, and there's nothing travelling through it. But there's also a sense of excitement, of anticipation—of not knowing what lies beyond that horizon.' She looked at him shyly. 'Does that sound very stupid?'

'No,' he said, sipping his coffee, and watching her with those inscrutable, beautiful grey eyes. 'But the horizon is only about two miles away.'

'Really?' she blinked.

'It only takes about fifteen minutes to get to the horizon,' he nodded. 'Maybe you'll reach your own horizons equally quickly.'

'Maybe,' she said quietly.

He drained his coffee with a quick, dismissive movement, and stood up.

'Things have happened in rather a rush,' he said with a quirk of his mouth. 'You don't really know very much about this boat. Well, I'm going to start making a sailor of you, Thursday Hunter.'

She rose rather apprehensively. 'If you say so,' she agreed halfheartedly.

'I do say so. We'll start by going over the boat inch by inch.' He took her arm in a strong grip, and led her over the complicated-looking foredeck to the prow. 'This is the sharp end,' he informed her with a poker-face. 'We'll work our way to the blunt end, and then have some breakfast.'

By eleven o'clock, two days later, the sun was high, and it had become beautifully hot. *Seaspray* was sailing briskly along through the leaping waves, and there was little to do to keep her on course. Thursday had curled up in the shade of the coach-roof with a novel, and Brendan was sunbathing on the afterdeck. He had stripped to a black Speedo so narrow and thin that Thursday had flushed. He had noted the pinkness of her cheeks with an ironic smile, and had commented, 'This is more than I would normally have worn to sunbathe in.' She looked up from her book absently. Did that mahogany tan, then, extend all over his body? She suddenly found herself thinking thoughts that were intimate enough to raise the blood to her cheeks again, and she bit her lip angrily. Whatever sort of morals she had had *before* she lost her memory, she was no loose woman *now*.

Yet she could not help staring at Brendan. What a magnificent physique he had! He was as perfect as some Classical bronze athlete. No—more robust, perhaps.

There was so little spare flesh on his big frame that each muscle, from the thickest to the most delicate, was outlined under the mahogany velvet of his skin. He had a chest and arms that might have belonged to Mars; yet for all his size, that body was neat and lithe. The long trickle of dark, copper-highlighted hair that descended in a wide triangle from his chest down to the black costume did not conceal the definition of his stomach muscles. Would that beautiful body be hard, she wondered, like oak or bronze? Probably, she thought. Hard and warm. The thought made her shiver for some reason, and she looked away from the mysterious black triangle of his costume hastily, and tried to concentrate on her book.

Her own body, she thought bitterly, was no match for his. Next to his perfection, she was blotchy, a scarred and mottled thing, so thin that her ribs showed through her burned skin. She had wanted to wear the lilac bikini she had chosen at Tom's store, but at the last minute shame had prevented her. She had settled for the long-sleeved shirt she had put on at dawn, and a pair of towelling shorts. She contemplated her legs morosely. They might have been pretty, but for the cross-hatching of cuts across the shins and around the fullness of her calves. There were scratches and cuts all over her feet, too, and in the pinkness of her heels. She glanced up resentfully at Brendan's magnificent body again.

At least she knew a bit more about him now. As she had suspected, he had built *Seaspray* himself. He was the master of a yacht-building yard in Sydney, and *Seaspray* was one of his most successful designs. A succession of colleagues going sick had necessitated that he deliver this yacht to its new owner personally—a professional yacht-racer called Michael Collins, based in San Francisco.

'With the price *Seaspray*'s going for,' he had told her laconically, 'I couldn't afford to jeopardise the sale.' In San Francisco he was going to pick up another boat, a century-old schooner called *Whiplash*, which he had decided to buy as a hobby.

'An expensive sort of hobby,' she had commented, and he had shrugged.

'My business is very successful. I don't believe in hoarding money away—it's there to be used and enjoyed. And *Whiplash* happens to be one of the most beautiful things in the world.'

'Oh,' she had commented, strangely chastened. After that, she had paid especial care to *Seaspray*, and had been at first impressed, then astounded, by the sheer mastery with which she had been designed and built. Every detail was perfect, each vibrating muscle and sinew of the yacht exactly placed, fulfilling its function with strength and grace and beauty. Every hatch, every strip of wood or brass, every perfect component of the perfect whole, every rope, fitted wonderfully into place. There was little doubt that Brendan Kavanagh was successful. Even if he never sold a yacht, he would be successful—completely successful, in that he had created a masterpiece.

She glanced at his hands, resting peacefully at his sides. Strong hands, yet also delicate hands—the sure fingers of a surgeon or a musician. Hands that could grip like a steel vice. Hands that could caress with exquisite gentleness. Again, that shiver passed through her.

He had been born in England, the son of an Irish father and a Scottish mother, a mixture which explained the stern beauty of his face and the sensuous curve of that fascinating mouth. He had left England some six or seven years ago to join the boatyard in Sydney. Within two years, he had risen to be a full partner, and when the elderly master of the yard had died, Brendan had bought the shares from his widow. With his finger on the pulse of modern yacht design, and with a mixture of hard Scots business sense and a Celtic flair of imagination, he had turned the business into a roaring success. He had not said so, but she knew he was a rich man. Not ostentatiously rich—he wore no jewellery at all, and his clothes were simple and masculine, rather than effeminately fashionable—but with that confident poise that only success can breed.

'Do you miss England?' she asked suddenly, and he smiled.

'Yes. Australia's beautiful—but I miss the greenness of England. The mistiness and softness of the landscape.' His eyes were suddenly soft. 'I miss autumn evenings, and log fires, and chestnuts. All the sentimental things, I guess.' He shrugged, obviously wanting to put the mood aside.

'I never thought of you as the sentimental type,' she teased gently. 'I had you down as a modern version of Captain Bligh.'

Brendan glanced up at her with a strange half-smile on his lips.

'I've been rather rough with you, haven't I?' he said quietly, raising himself up on one elbow to look at her face. 'I guess you think pretty badly of me.'

'You were a little—unkind at times,' she admitted. 'I didn't like you any less for it, though. I was presuming on your time and patience. I still am.'

'No, Thursday, you're not.' His eyes were still gentle, but his face was serious. 'I was overreacting badly. I'm not in so much of a rush that I couldn't spare a week or two to help another human being in distress. The truth is——' He paused, looking away, and she watched him, her chin cupped in her palm.

'What is the truth?' she prompted quietly. He smiled, looking almost uncomfortable.

'Well,' he sighed, 'the fact is that at first I was kind of wary of you. Scared, would be a more honest way of putting it.'

'*Scared?*' she gaped, astounded by this new insight into him.

'Yeah,' he nodded with a shamefaced smile. 'Not of you specifically—but of what you represented.'

'And what did I represent?'

'Someone vulnerable. And female. Someone who was going to need looking after, who would make demands on my emotions. Someone to be responsible for.'

'Does responsibility scare you that much?' she asked, and waved at the yacht. 'It doesn't look like it to me.'

'Emotional responsibility is something else,' he said softly, and the depth in his eyes made her shiver involuntarily. 'I simply wasn't ready for any emotional supercargo, Thursday. I had planned this trip simple, technically uncluttered, emotionally independent. And the minute I lifted your body off the sand at Hunter, I knew that I was picking up a whole new world of emotional ties and responsibilities.'

She digested this in silence, not knowing whether to be pleased or not by what he had shown her of his feelings.

'And now?' she queried. 'Do you regret having taken me on—with my little world of ties and responsibilities?'

'No,' he said simply, and his smile went straight to her heart. 'You're kind of fun, Thursday Hunter. And you've been very good for me.'

'You've been very good for me,' she said, almost in a whisper, as though frightened of the feelings that his words were setting off in her. She had never been so close to him. Suddenly wanting to change the subject, she put on a bright smile.

'You never told me where you grew up.'

'Mostly in East Anglia,' he told her. 'My father had an architectural firm in Norwich. That's where we lived until I was eight.'

'And then?'

'That's when my parents died,' he said quietly. 'Within a few months of each other.'

'Oh—I am sorry——'

'It's all long gone now.' He smiled wryly. 'I had some rough times at first. They put me in a local children's home for a year or two. Then I had a succession of foster-homes. It wasn't too bad,' he grinned, noting her expression of dismay. 'Most people were very kind to me. People are in that part of the world.'

'It's all very flat and windy, isn't it?' she said, and he looked at her quizzically.

'More or less. How do you know?'

'Oh, I don't have any memories of it,' she sighed. 'That's what I call "dead knowledge"—the sort of things I must have learned somewhere, but don't actually *know*—if you see what I mean. Anyway,' she said apologetically, 'never mind that. Tell me what you were like as a boy.'

He laughed, amused by her serious tone.

'I was a wicked little creature, I suppose. And I hated school. I was always playing hookey so that I could build model ships and sail them on the local pond.'

'Promise showing early?'

'I guess so. I still build model ships and sail them on my pond. I've had a big ornamental pool made in my garden, with osiers and lotus lilies and pampas grass. It does very nicely as a testing ground for my prototypes.'

She smiled at the image of him sailing model yachts on his pond, his masculine face intent.

'It sounds lovely, Brendan. God, I wish I could remember my own past! It's so terribly frustrating not knowing where you come from——' She broke off, shaking her head bitterly.

'I understand,' he said quietly. 'It's very frustrating living with someone who has no past, I assure you. I'd love to know more about you.'

'You would?'

'If you were a mathematical equation, we could let your past be X, and then work it all out with logic. You must have known how to sail, Thursday. And that implies that somebody must have taught you.' He fixed her with his wide grey eyes. 'I'd guess that one of your parents must have taught you how to sail. Probably a father. And that suggests that your father was somehow nautical. Or even Naval.' He cocked his head. 'Have you any memories of a father who was in the Navy?'

Something stirred deep in her subconscious, and she sat, frozen, the blood draining from her face. The fingers of her mind grasped after the elusive shadow until she gasped with the effort.

'Thursday!' Suddenly he was at her side, his fingers biting into her arm. 'Have you remembered something?'

'I thought—oh, it's gone,' she groaned. 'There was something there—at least I think there was. But it's slipped away.'

'Are you all right?'

'I'm just—just a bit faint,' she said uncertainly. 'I—I think I'd better lie down a while. This sun is making me a bit giddy.'

He helped her to her feet, his face concerned.

'Well, at least we seem to have touched something there,' he said seriously. 'When we make Hawaii, we'll get hold of a copy of the Navy List, and go through the names of all the captains in the right age-bracket. Okay?'

'Okay.' She leaned gratefully against the power of his shoulder, aware of the hot velvet of his skin against her own. He tilted her chin up, and pressed a firm kiss on her lips, almost making her buckle at the knees; and then he was helping her down to her cabin.

She was asleep almost before her head touched the pillow.

CHAPTER FOUR

THE next days passed peacefully, in sunshine and calm seas. She was still weak, and feeling the strain of her forgotten ordeal, and she slept a lot; and when she thought Brendan wasn't looking, lay in the sun for cautious periods. It took her some time to realise quite how badly shocked she had been. The panic of awakening into a strange world without her memory had driven all her gentler feelings into the background. Now, in the utter peace of the beautiful white yacht, on calm seas that sparkled in warm sunlight, they returned. Her femininity began to reassert itself—at first intermittently, in the shape of a keener interest in what she wore and how she looked—and then with a rush of half-remembered memories about ways of doing her hair, ways of wearing her clothes, ways of treating her skin.

If she looked at herself in the little cabin mirror and tried to think what to do with her appearance, her mind seemed to go into a kind of paralysis. But she found that if she relaxed, did things instinctively and without thought, actions came back to her. The way she used to comb her thick blonde hair back on one side and fasten it in a golden wave; the way she used to rub cream into her silky skin; the way she would touch her lips with the lightest brushing of lip-gloss.

To her annoyance, she found that she hadn't bothered to buy many of the things she really needed— hair-clips, make-up accessories, and the like. But during her rushed trip to the chemist on Viti Levu, she had at least equipped herself with some basic essentials, like skin creams, shampoo, a few plastic packs of mascara and gloss. She had been in a very unfeminine phase then. And also so embittered about her disfigured skin that to think of vanities like make-up had seemed ridiculous.

She began to have faint hopes that the ugly patches of burned skin would fade. When she studied her face in her mirror, she noticed that the edges of the burned areas, once sharply defined against the clear honey of her skin, had begun to blur and soften. It was an interesting face, she thought absently, staring at it without vanity. The mouth was soft and full, a perfect pink leaf whose upper and lower lips were almost exactly the same size. Her chin was a pretty oval, her nose short and straight; but it was her eyes which were perhaps her best point. Widely-spaced and fringed with lashes so thick and dark that they didn't need mascara to look dramatic, they were a clear, deep green with large pupils. Her eyebrows were perhaps too thick—yet their dark curves gave character to her face, and she didn't have the heart to try and narrow them down. Under the long fall of her hair, her forehead was high and smooth, the one part of her face that had escaped burning. And her hair was thick and heavy enough to be almost a burden to her in the hot weather. Washing it in salt water made it stiff and dry, and she had asked Brendan for permission to rinse it in fresh water from their tanks—normally only used for drinking and cooking.

'If you must,' he had agreed unenthusiastically. But when she had emerged after washing it, to dry it in the sun, she had noticed him staring at the silky golden tresses that fluttered in the light breeze.

As for the rest of her body—well, that was something she didn't care to think about. The top of her body had caught the worst of the sun, and across her shoulders and breasts the skin had been scorched. It was still peeling a little at the edges of the raw areas. Her shins, too, had taken a battering—and the only part of her body which was unblemished was the part she couldn't possibly expose—the smooth curve of her hips, her loins and bottom. The unfairness of it made her shake her head.

And so she had stuck to loose T-shirts and frocks or shorts. The clothing she had selected at Tom Kandavu's store was, she now realised with disappointment, scarcely elegant—consisting mostly of practical cotton or towelling beachwear.

Yet some instinct prompted her to do the best she could with what she had. She wanted to look pretty, she supposed, because there was a very attractive man on board. But also because she knew that careful presentation might minimise—or distract from—the ugliness of her skin. So she compromised.

The prettiest of her T-shirts was a light, loose, bamboo-patterned affair. She knotted it carefully at one side to show her satiny midriff yet conceal her burned shoulders. And she combed her hair back in a shining sweep, securing it with the plain, practical bobby-pins that were her only hair-care aid. She examined herself in the cabin mirror. If you didn't look too closely— well, if you were on a galloping horse—she might have been some starlet stepping on to the beach at Antibes or Cannes. Then she shrugged with a sigh. Who was she fooling? Despondent, she went through into the galley to make lunch.

When she came up on to the deck with the bowls of soup she had made, Brendan was just aft of the coach-roof, staring at the horizon ahead through binoculars. He turned to look at her, his grey eyes flicking from her face down to her legs.

'What's the big occasion?' he enquired, taking his

bowl with a nod of thanks.

'Nothing,' she shrugged, secretly pleased that he had noticed the care she had taken. 'I just thought I was beginning to look a bit tatty, that's all.'

'Yes, you were rather,' he agreed bluntly. 'Mmmm, this soup is good. It's not tinned, is it?'

'Of course not! I used the last of our vegetables from Lautoka—and some stock cubes. And a few herbs. That's all.'

'How did you know which herbs to use?' he asked, one black eyebrow quirking interrogatively.

'I'm not sure,' she mused. 'It was just there. I guess it's one of those things you don't forget—like riding a bicycle.'

'Or making love,' he suggested calmly.

She almost choked over her soup, feeling her face go red. But he didn't seem to notice.

'It's very good, in any case. You must be quite a cook to have concocted this out of the scraps in the galley.'

'It's just soup,' she protested, inwardly delighted at his praise.

'My mother used to say there's no such thing as "just soup",' he said, favouring her with one of his rare smiles. It was a beautiful smile, she reflected, that pulled the sensuous mouth into a fascinating curve.

'Soup is an art,' he said. 'So is looking good,' he added, surveying her figure appreciatively. Not knowing quite what to say, she spooned soup into her mouth with downcast eyes. 'It might even be worth buying some decent food in Canton,' he said.

'Canton?'

'Canton Island. It's our next stop—just over the horizon. Look—see those clouds in the distance?' She nodded, looking at the far-away puffs of white on the blue horizon. 'You only get those clouds over land.' He

glanced at his watch. 'We should be there by one
o'clock. If you like, you can do the provisioning.
There's a market in Lewistown—and it'll be a good six
days to Hawaii.'

'I'd like that,' she nodded. 'If you trust me, that is.'

'There are only two of us in this boat,' he said
austerely. 'And right now there's about half a mile of
ocean underneath us.' He looked at her with level grey
eyes. 'I have to trust you—don't I?'

The Lewistown market was a bright and bustling affair,
thronged with Island women in long, gaudily-coloured
print dresses. She had climbed the steep hill from the
yacht-mole, past the long row of bamboo and palm-leaf
houses, leaving Brendan to sort out the technical details
of *Seaspray*'s refuelling.

Most of the fruits and vegetables arrayed on the
crowded stands were unfamiliar to her. Some, though,
she recognised—artichokes, avocado pears, squashes of
every description. Others she could guess at—yams,
banyan fruits, eggplants, pumpkins. Bargaining with
the vociferous storekeepers was a mixture of silent
comedy and tragic mime. As a general rule, she offered
half of what they initially requested, then let herself be
badgered into parting with a few pennies more. Within
a short while, she had collected two huge basketsfull of
glossy fruit and vegetables. One of the stalls was selling
fresh fish, and after pondering over the unlikely-looking
delights of squid, octopus and sea-urchins, she settled
for several gleaming tunny-fish and a glistening
barracuda—which the eager little store-keeper assured
her was excellent eating. He threw in a wicker basket to
carry her purchases away in, and she struggled back
down the hill towards the mole where *Seaspray* was
anchored. There was a small deep-freeze in the galley,
which she had noted disapprovingly was filled with

oven-roast chips, cartons of ice-cream, and various convenience foods. The fish would keep nicely in there.

She heaved her prizes aboard *Seaspray*. She could see Brendan standing at the end of the pier, a tall figure talking to a grizzled old European in a faded nautical-looking hat. She packed the food away, working with neat, efficient movements in the cramped spaces of the galley. She had grown amazingly accustomed to life on the boat; she had long since stopped banging her head on things or barking her shins on things, and she adjusted her balance instinctively to counterpoise the constant movement of the yacht. That done, she peered over the spray hood. He was still talking to the grizzled old character, and she cast a longing glance at the rickety-looking shop on the wharf, which bore a sign reading ELLIS PEARSON BROS GNRL DLRS & TRADING STORE. Paul Taveuni had pressed a moderate supply of money 'just in case' on her in Lautoka, and Ellis Pearson Bros looked as though they would have the hair-clips and things she needed. Her mind made up, she trotted down the gangplank, across the wharf, and into the tempting darkness of the slightly ramshackle shop. Her heart lifted at the racks of beautiful print dresses and skirts. A long-buried feminine instinct to have some pretty clothes was suddenly emerging very rapidly indeed!

She must have enjoyed beautiful clothes in her former life. Well, after all, what woman didn't? What had her tastes run to? Pearls and twin-sets? Hardly. Jeans and scuffed tennis-shoes? Unlikely again. And what would she have made of these brilliant prints in her pre-memory loss days? She sorted happily through the rustling garments. Well, they were a godsend right now, that was for sure!

She was out again in half an hour, carrying several packages, just in time to meet Brendan at *Seaspray*'s mooring. The sun was high, and a light breeze was ruffling the unbelievably clear water of the little bay.

With no fuss, they slipped the white yacht's mooring ropes, hoisted her sails, and sailed out of the bay into the afternoon.

Thursday helped Brendan perform various routine tasks during the afternoon; but the heat was lazy, and they both slept on the deck for an hour, waking as the sun had begun to dip towards the horizon, beginning to gild the sea ahead. Canton Island had slipped into the water behind them, and only its little tablecloth of white cloud could be seen. A wide feathering of cirrus extended high in the sky overhead, and it promised to be a beautiful sunset.

She went down into the galley to prepare their supper. Since Brendan's praise—unexpected and unlooked-for praise—over her soup, Thursday had been looking at the galley with new and speculative eyes. Like everything else that Brendan had designed, it was beautifully logical and well organised. The little gas oven set beneath the mast was suddenly filled with possibilities in her eyes. From the dim recesses of her mind, cooking ideas and processes were beginning to drift. Thoughtfully, she began to ponder out a menu. On deck, Brendan was hauling up some more canvas to take advantage of the last breeze of the afternoon; in this warm ocean, the setting of the sun usually betokened two or three hours of calm, when the sea would be as still and flat as an English millpond. She nodded to herself. Nothing too complicated at first— tomato soup, followed by fish. Good. She lifted the chopping-board from its hook, and set to work.

The sun was low by the time she was ready. She slipped into her cabin to put on the first of her purchases from the trading store, an island dress that she had fallen in love with at first sight. It was made from some kind of raw silk, in an unusual, kimono-like cut. The top folded over her breasts, and was secured by a slim cord that also acted as a belt round her waist. The colours were pretty—a pale pastel yellow with a patterning of yellow and gold leaves. Yet the chaste Japanese-style effect was deceptive. The past few days had filled Thursday's figure out, and the whispering material clung to her skin as she moved, outlining her figure in tantalising glimpses. The top in particular gave her a few qualms. She didn't want to spoil it by wearing a bra—but on the other hand it did rather cling to the soft, uptilted curves of her bosom. What was more, she had to be careful not to let the fold slip forward and reveal the creamy swell of her breast. The effect was undeniably sexy—but so deliciously feminine, and such a glamorous change from the cotton T-shirts that had been the peak of her fashion achievements so far that she couldn't resist it. She brushed her hair back into two gleaming waves, secured them with the plastic butterfly-decorated clips that were all Ellis Pearson Bros could supply, and looked at herself shyly. She was almost unrecognisable as the drab girl from the hospital! She made her lips shine with a touch of gloss, decided against mascara, and went up to serve dinner. Brendan's reaction would tell her whether her outfit was a success or not.

There was a fold-out melamine table in the cockpit which made a convenient on-deck dining-table in the seating area. On it she spread the second of her purchases from Ellis Pearson Bros—a pretty green-and-white tablecloth, native cotton block-printed with simple, charming pictures of fish and flowers.

Brendan stared at her in surprise.

'Where did that come from?' he demanded.

'I bought it on Canton,' she said calmly. 'I got tired of eating off the melamine.'

'I wasn't referring to the tablecloth,' he retorted, his eyes taking in her dress with shameless interest, lingering with arrogant flattery at her breasts and hips. 'You look like Mata Hari!'

Not sure whether to be flattered or disappointed, she laid out the knives, forks and spoons, and nodded to the seats. 'Sit down,' she invited. 'I'll bring it up.'

The sky had become a magnificent canvas of fiery reds and yellows, fading into lilac and dim purple up above. The orange ball of the sun sent a long track of glittering rubies across the calm water towards them, and the heat of the day had given way to the still warmth of late afternoon. She brought the soup up from the galley, rather anxious as to what he would say. The recipe she had evolved was not exactly conventional. Where it had come from, she wasn't certain. She put the tureens on the table, and Brendan stared at them with wide grey eyes. Each bowl was surmounted by a golden-brown dome of puff pastry, a deliciously crisp shell that steamed lightly.

'What is it?' he asked in astonishment.

'Tomato soup,' she told him coolly, and taking her courage in her hands, broke through the crust with her spoon. A mouthwatering aroma of tomato, onion, garlic and herbs floated out. Within the crunchy shell, the soup was hot and exquisitely savoury. Brendan followed suit after a moment's hesitation, and tasted the soup within. He looked up at her in amazement.

'Where on earth did you learn to make this?' he asked. 'It's delicious!'

'It should have white wine and celery in it as well,' she said, trying not to show her delight at his pleasure, 'but I couldn't get anything like that on Canton.'

'How do you know it should have had those things in it?' he asked curiously.

She shook her head.

'I don't know. I suppose I must have made this before.' The pastry crunched crisply against the spoon, yet melted in the mouth—and the soup was a delicate, savoury delight. It was evident from Brendan's expression that he simply couldn't believe it. After a few more mouthfuls, he laid his spoon down to stare at her with deep grey eyes.

'You never cease to amaze me, Thursday,' he said quietly. 'Why, this is—well, it's Cordon Bleu cooking!'

'Hardly,' she smiled. 'It was very easy—I just baked the pastry on to the tureens.'

'Believe me,' he said firmly, 'for cooking at sea, this is exceptional. Wait.' He dabbed at his mouth with his napkin, rose hastily, and disappeared down the companionway. When he re-emerged, he was holding a bottle of white wine and a corkscrew. He grinned at her. 'I'd almost forgotten about these—I stowed a few bottles under my bunk before I left Sydney. If the rest of the meal is going to match this soup, we're going to have to do it justice.' He uncorked the bottle deftly, and poured the amber liquid into two glasses. The setting sun sent shafts of fire into the wine and he smiled at her, the sunset putting amethyst glints into his beautiful eyes. 'It's not really cool enough, I'm afraid—but here's to you, Thursday.'

The warmth of the wine had released the full fruitiness of its flavour. It was an excellent German white, tasting of grapes and summer, and it slid down Thursday's throat like liquid gold. Suddenly she felt very happy. A more wonderful setting, she reflected, could scarcely have been found.

'There's not a restaurant in the world that can boast décor like this,' she smiled, gesturing at the sheets of fire in the west, the golden sea. Brendan crunched pastry with relish, and grinned at her. She felt closer to him than she had ever been, and Paul Taveuni's words

echoed through her mind—'I shouldn't be surprised if
you ended up fast friends.' She toasted the sentiment
silently, relishing the sweet fragrance of the wine.

'That was a minor masterpiece,' he said, putting
down his spoon. 'When I lifted you off Hunter Island,
Thursday, I never expected to see you looking like this.'
His eyes dropped to her breast, and she glanced at
herself involuntarily. Her breasts were making two taut
peaks against the fine material, and she adjusted the silk
with a slight flush. Brendan smiled with gentle irony.

'You're very unsure of yourself, aren't you?' he said
quietly.

'Why do you say that?'

'You remind me of——' He paused, his dark,
passionate face quietly amused. 'Of a seventeen-year-
old girl at her first ball. You had the courage to choose
a beautiful and rather daring dress,' he said, raising his
glass to her, 'but you haven't quite got the courage to
wear it. You're always worried in case you're revealing
too much.' He drank some wine, his eyes on hers.

'Isn't that natural?' she asked, looking down.

'A more poised woman,' he shrugged, 'would take a
certain pleasure in being admired.'

'It's not very easy to be poised with a complete
stranger,' she reminded him quietly.

'Complete? Not quite.' He smiled into her eyes with
breathtaking mockery. 'I've seen you naked, don't
forget, my dear Thursday. I washed you, and changed
your clothes, and put you to bed. I feel quite fatherly
towards you.' The wicked sparkle in his smile
contradicted his words. Whatever he was feeling
towards her, it certainly wasn't fatherly!

Suddenly very uncomfortable, she stood up to take
the tureens. She had the feeling that those splendid grey
eyes, with their amethyst depths, had dispensed with her
silk dress and were studying her naked body.

'I'm going to have to learn to live without vanity,' she said stiffly, the orange glow of the dying sun setting fire to her long hair.

'I would have thought that would be impossible for a woman,' he said, passing her his bowl.

'Do you have such a low opinion of women?'

'Not at all,' he smiled. 'A certain quantity of self-respect—call it vanity if you like—is essential to surviving in this world. But why should you have to do without it?'

'I would have thought that was obvious,' she said, turning her face away. 'I look like a circus clown.'

'If you're fishing for compliments,' he said acidly, 'then you're a lot stupider than I gave you credit for.' She met his eyes. 'Thursday,' he said more kindly, 'stop worrying about yourself. It's only a week or two since you got those burns, you know. They'll heal.'

She picked up the plates in silence and went down to the galley. She had baked the barracuda, then sliced the firm white meat into thin ovals, frying them lightly with a little garlic and a tarragon-like herb she had picked up on one of the stalls. Now she arranged the delicate slices of fish with sweet potatoes, roasted pumpkin and slices of eggplant lightly fried in crisp batter, garnished the prettily-patterned dishes with a fine velouté sauce, and carried the plates up on deck with some fresh salad.

'I'm past being impressed,' said Brendan with a smile; and self-critical though she was, she had to admit that the meal was delicious. The sun had sunk by now, leaving the sky like a gigantic funeral pyre, a yellow and ruby glow deepening into a pale turquoise, and then into the velvety ultramarine of a South Pacific night. The first stars were already sparkling in the marvellously clear air. The musical gurgles of the sea around *Seaspray*'s prow were the only sound in the immense stillness.

Suddenly Brendan put his fork down, and laughed softly. She looked at him enquiringly in the soft light.

'You're astounding,' he said, still smiling. 'I was just thinking of it. Ten days ago you were just a naked pink thing sprawled on a rock. Tonight, you're sitting there, having cooked a superb meal, looking like a queen, as calm as though butter wouldn't melt in your mouth.' He shook his head, pouring her some more wine with an amused smile quirking his devastating mouth. 'I'm beginning to be rather glad I didn't sail past Hunter Island,' he said, and looked up at her speculatively. 'And I didn't know those native dresses could look quite so amazingly sexy,' he commented with light mockery.

She ate doggedly, eyes down.

'It wasn't meant to be sexy,' she said woodenly.

'But it is,' he smiled. 'And so are you.'

'You're kidding,' she said gauchely, looking up with quick attention.

'I wouldn't kid you,' he said gravely. 'You've got a habit of selling yourself short, Thursday Hunter. As a matter of fact,' he added, watching her with bright eyes, 'I think we're going to have to change your name again.'

The pink leaf of her mouth turned down in distaste, and she shook her silky hair back.

'I'd just begun to get used to Thursday,' she said, and there was a bitter undercurrent of self-mockery in her voice. He caught it, and was suddenly serious.

'Thursday,' he said with quiet seriousness, 'please don't think I'm ever mocking you about your amnesia.'

'Why not? It seems to be one of your favourite pastimes,' she said drily.

'God forbid! But "Thursday" seemed an appropriate name when you were a pale-faced child staring out of a hospital bed with wild eyes. Now, when you're looking like this,' he said, waving at her, 'it doesn't sound right any more.'

'Men must be very gullible,' she said ironically, finishing her meal. 'There's no difference between the woman in that bed and the woman sitting here—except a little soap and a few clothes.'

'That's not so,' he corrected with a faint smile on his commanding mouth. 'There's a lot more to it than that. But let's not argue. You were right—"Thursday" isn't a person's name. Wouldn't you like to be called something elese?' He rose, and stepped over the deck to light the red and green navigation lights.

'What would you suggest?' she asked with a slightly acid intonation, watching his tall, dark figure.

'How about Marina?' he suggested. 'That means "born of the sea".' He came over to sit next to her, an unexpectedly big figure, and smiled gently down at her.

'I don't know,' she said, suddenly dry-mouthed.

'Or Perdita?' he said softly, drawing his finger down her cheek. 'That's a pretty name.'

'What does it mean?' she asked huskily, suddenly acutely aware of his closeness to her.

' "Little lost one",' he told her, his eyes studying her face with intimate care.

'Those sound such lonely names,' she said, trying to smile nonchalantly. The odd thing was that the more Brendan smiled, the less she felt able to answer his smile. The quiet curve on those passionate, authoritative lips was doing strange things to her nerves.

'Desiderata, then,' he suggested, his deep voice caressing.

'What does that mean?' she asked, knowing the answer.

' "Desired one",' he said softly, caressing her cheek lightly with the back of his hand.

She was beginning to feel slightly breathless.

'I don't like that, either,' she said shakily. 'I'll just stick to "Thursday", I think—until my real name turns up.'

He laughed gently, and stood up, offering her his hand.

'Come—I want you to see something.'

His hand was warm and firm. She rose uncertainly, her heart beating a little faster. But as she turned and saw the moon, she let out an involuntary, 'Oh!' of delight.

It had risen out of the sea, a glorious golden disc set against the deep blue velvet of the east; a moon bigger and more luminous than anything she had ever dreamed of.

'It ought to be corny,' said Brendan, watching her shining eyes with a quiet smile. 'But somehow it isn't.'

'No,' she breathed, 'it's not.'

It glowed in the sky, like some pure and ineffably wonderful pearl—the earth's faithful companion in space, gilded with the light of the vanished sun.

'I wanted to show you something else, though,' he said, leading her to the stern. 'Look at the water.'

She leaned against the rail, blinking in disbelief. At first she thought it must be the reflection of the moon, but it wasn't. The sea itself seemed to be glowing. The dark surface of the water was bright with luminescence, and their wake was a glowing path of fairy diamonds and rubies and saphires.

'What is it?' she whispered half fearfully, spellbound by the magic of this ghostly burning sea.

'Phosphorescence,' he said. 'It's caused by millions upon millions of tiny plankton. I've seldom seen it so bright—but it's not uncommon in these waters.'

'It looks as though the sea's on fire,' she breathed. As she watched, the luminescence spread and widened around them until the whole sea seemed to be blazing red and green and gold and blue, a rippling, cold fire that flickered with an intense, almost mystical light. 'It's almost frightening,' she said in awe. The light the phosphorescence gave off was bright enough to be reflected in her emerald eyes as she stared at it in wonder, and Brendan watched her with a quiet smile on his face.

She looked down at the hull of the yacht, and saw that it, too, had been coated with living fire, as though by some fairy paintbrush. Brendan stooped, reaching through the taffrail, and dipped his hand into the rippling water. It came out blazing green and turquoise, and she took his fingers to study the phenomenon with wide eyes.

'Doesn't it burn?' she asked anxiously.

'No,' he smiled, 'no more than fireflies or glow-worms burn.' As she peered at his hand, she could see that the mysterious and beautiful glow was made up of millions of tiny pinpoints of light that flickered and faded as she watched. The glow went out slowly, leaving his hand cold and dripping with salt water. Thursday found that she was still holding his hand in both her own, staring into his palm as though she were a gypsy fortune-teller. She let his fingers go, suddenly shy.

'Tell me my fortune,' he commanded softly.

She turned to walk away, her heart beating, but he reached out and drew her back, turning her to face him. 'What a shy thing you are,' he murmured, his splendid face amused. He brushed the golden hair back that had escaped from its clip and drifted across her forehead. 'I'm not going to eat you!'

She looked up into his face uncertainly. She had never realised before quite how stunning his male beauty was. His face was moulded with a stern authority that was almost intimidating. The straight nose and level brows spoke of a commanding, cold nature; yet there was grey fire in those deep eyes, and passion lurked in the curve of his mouth. It was his mouth, she thought nervously, which was the most disturbing thing about that face—it turned up at the corners with a mocking quirk, yet the full lower lip was exciting, sensuous.

'I'd better make some coffee,' she said shakily.

'I wonder,' he said, smiling lazily down at her, 'whether you were right.'

'About what?' she ventured.

'About never being able to forget how to ride a bicycle. Or sail a boat. Or make love.'

The hard angles of his cheekbones were softened by a quick, teasing smile. Then he stooped and kissed her.

CHAPTER FIVE

His mouth was hard and firm against hers. His kiss was brief and challenging, and the harsh pressure of his lips shocked her into opening her emerald eyes wide. The delicate flower of her mouth felt bruised, and she parted her lips breathlessly.

'Brendan,' she faltered, 'I don't——'

'Don't tell me you've never been kissed by a man before,' he said, his eyes sparkling with wicked amusement.

She tried to free her arms from his grip, but he merely pulled her closer to him with a quiet laugh. His chest and stomach were hard against her body—she fancied she could almost feel his heart beating through the thin silk of her dress.

'You're delicious,' he said in a low growl, staring down at her with eyes which had begun to burn with a bright grey light. 'Your mouth is as soft and sweet as a frangipani blossom.'

She tried to struggle away as he bent his lips to hers again, but he was too strong.

'No,' she said nervously, trying to turn her head aside, 'Let me go, I——'

Firmly, his mouth took hers again, his full, sensuous lower lip pressing hers apart, and her protests were muffled. She struggled in panic, but he merely held her closer to him, so that her full breasts were crushed against the hardness of his chest, and he could feel the length of her thighs against his under the raw silk. He released her mouth, and she gasped in mixed fear and anger as he slowly, deliberately, kissed the side of her neck.

'Let me go, you——'

'What?' he asked lazily, holding her close and gazing down at her with a mocking smile.

'You *bully*!' she gritted.

'You schoolgirl,' he smiled. And this time his kiss was fierce and rough, an invasion that brooked no resistance or disobedience. His hands dropped to the small of her back, pressing her hips forwards against him. For an instant, desire blazed in her, then she fought it back. She put her hands desperately against his hard chest, and thrust herself away, gasping, her thick golden hair tumbling forwards around her face.

'You lack manners!' she snapped fiercely at his laughing face, and spun away, tugging the loosened top of her dress closed over her breasts. She stopped at the other side of the stern, clutching the rail with trembling hands and staring with angry, unseeing eyes at the golden pearl of the moon.

Brendan stepped up lightly behind her and took her shoulders gently in his hands. She tried to shake them off, but he held her firm, drawing her back so that she had no option but to lean against his tall body.

'Do you know what you look like in that dress?' he asked softly, his breath warm against her neck.

'An easy pick-up?' she asked with venomous sarcasm.

'It was you who picked me up,' he reminded her, the smile audible in his deep voice.

'I didn't think you were the sort of man who would force his attentions on a helpless woman,' she retorted.

'Force? Who would have the heart to force a beautiful rosebud to open?' he mocked gently. 'The sun will do that by and by.' She felt his lips brush the silky skin at the side of her slender neck, and an involuntary shiver ran through her. Feeling it, he laughed softly, and slipped his arms around her, pulling her even closer against him, so that her head was resting against his cheek.

'The moon is lovely,' he said quietly, his powerful arms holding her just beneath the soft swell of her breasts.

'The moon is lucky to be on her own,' she retorted. But the nearness of his body and the warmth of his breath on her temple was doing strange things to her breathing.

'Why not relax?' he smiled. 'Don't you trust me, Thursday?'

'Not when you insist on kissing me against my wishes,' she answered coolly. He relaxed his arms, allowing her to twist round, then treacherously pulled her close again, so that their faces were almost touching. She could see the golden moon reflected in the brilliant depths of his grey eyes.

'Is this against your wishes?' he asked softly—and his third kiss took her senses by storm. As he tasted the inner sweetness of her mouth, she could feel herself opening to him, like some beautiful flower that was unfolding, petal by delicate petal, under the caress of the sun.

Feelings that were utterly strange to her began to swell, rise, flame within her. At first she tried to question them, and then desire was alight in her. She slid her arms around his neck, her mouth beginning to respond to his. Her lips fluttered against his timidly; and as though her inexpert caress had inflamed him, he crushed her to him, plundering her lips with a desire that seemed to scald her, that burned her tender senses. Nothing could have prepared her for the intensity and power of Brendan Kavanagh's kisses, and when at last he released her unwillingly, she was weak and shaky. With astonishment, he saw the glistening tear seep from under the thick, dark fringe of her tightly-closed lashes.

'What on earth is wrong?' he asked. 'Why are you crying, child?'

'Because I know why you're doing this,' she choked, the bruised pink leaf of her perfect mouth quivering. 'You think I'll be an easy conquest because—because I'm disfigured!'

'Disfigured?' He stared down at the pale oval of her face in amazement, then in anger. 'You're not disfigured, you little fool,' he said almost roughly.

'I know I am,' she said fiercely, opening eyes like wet emeralds to glare at him. 'I can see my face in the mirror—my shoulders, my breasts—I'm as ugly as a leper!'

She tried to thrust herself out of his arms, but he jerked her savagely back.

'Ugly?' he snarled, his dark brows lowering. 'Why, you idiot, you're beautiful! For God's sake, don't you know that?'

'Please don't try and be kind to me,' she said icily, shaking tears like diamonds off the satiny skin of her upper cheeks. 'I'm not blind. And no matter what's happened to me, Brendan, I——'

She broke off with a gasp as his strong fingers clenched in her thick hair, pulling her to face him with brutal power.

'Listen to me,' he said softly, his grey eyes narrowed to a steely glitter, 'you seem determined to play the tragic heroine, Thursday. Well, you're wrong. You're beautiful, young woman—no matter whether you've been burned or not. Do you hear me?' He jerked at her hair, hurting her cruelly. 'You're beautiful, damn you!'

He stared down into her upturned face, his proud nostrils flaring. 'Why, your eyes are like the jewels in an Empress's crown—and your mouth——' He kissed it roughly, his man's lips rough against the petal-like skin. '—it's like hot silk. You fool! Disfigured?' He crushed her to him, burying his face in the thickness of her hair, and she clung to him with arms that were weak, a terrible ache deep in her heart. 'Your hair smells of summer,' he groaned, his voice husky. 'It's thick and warm and beautiful——'

'Brendan,' she whispered tremulously, intoxicated by his words, by the desire she could so plainly hear in his thrilling voice. He let her go, and she leaned back against the rail, suddenly burning hot, her skin feeling as though it was on fire. He watched her with hungry eyes as she threw her delicate head back and shook her golden hair loose in the moonlight. The silk dress was loose, and she knew he could see the tender curve of her breasts, but she no longer cared. Their eyes met, and she smiled at him shakily.

'I won't ask you if you meant that,' she said softly. 'But thank you for saying it, Brendan. It means a lot to me.'

'I could go on in greater detail,' he said meaningfully, looking down at the swell of her hips in the cool silk of the Island dress. 'Your legs, for instance—they're as graceful as a dancer's, long and slender. Whatever you were before you lost your memory, Thursday, you've got all the grace and poise of a gazelle.' He smiled, reaching out his hand to her. 'Come and sit with me.' The silk of her dress whispered confidingly as she sat next to him in the shelter of the spray hood. He pulled her gently to him, brushing her neck with his lips, and the muted fire leaped into flickering life in her again.

'No,' she whispered, but she couldn't stop him. His

kisses moved into the soft hollow of her throat, and she arched her neck in ecstasy as he pulled her to him.

Her soft lips were parted for him, but now he was in no hurry. With maddening slowness, he kissed her temples, the silky skin of her upper cheeks, the fluttering lids of her eyes. And when at last his mouth took hers, she met him eagerly.

Thursday was conscious of her own clumsiness; her lips were inexpert, shy against the harsh power of his kiss—yet her awkwardness seemed only to arouse him more. She felt herself melting in the furnace of his desire, her identity dissolving in a mutual flame that was consuming them both. She had never dreamed that in a kiss there could be so much shared, so much exchanged—such a stunning oneness of two wills and minds. She was one with Brendan—as inseparable from his substance as a river flowing into the sea, or the flames of two candles blending.

His hand slid the silk of her dress aside, cupping the fullness of her breast tenderly, his thumb brushing her nipple in a way that sent liquid fire coursing through her veins. The wind blew gently in her loosened hair, and she slid back against the seat weakly, pushing his hand gently away, murmuring, 'No, Brendan, please——'

He smiled at her, his eyes burning with a fire that thrilled her. 'Am I going too fast for you?' he asked softly. 'You're so beautiful, Thursday, so tender.'

'All this is very new to me, Brendan,' she whispered. 'I don't think I've ever kissed a man before.'

'I don't think you have, either,' he said, tracing the beautiful line of her cheek with his finger. 'You're as shy as a schoolgirl. And as innocent.'

'I don't know what to do,' she said, hot with shyness, looking away. 'I suppose you think me very gauche.'

'Not gauche,' he said in a low voice, his passionate mouth gentle. 'Just inexperienced. You don't even know how to kiss a man.'

'Is there a way?' she asked in some surprise.

'I'll show you,' he smiled, and leaned forward. Now he did not press his mouth to hers, but merely brushed it with his lips, a caress that was as exciting as it was gentle. She looked at him with wide green eyes, and he smiled quietly, then kissed her again. Her lips seemed to cling to his as he moved back again, and she dropped her thickly-fringed eyes to study his mouth. His arms slipped around her shoulders, drawing her to him, and their mouths met with a profound tenderness that shook her. What had been a fierce flame now became a sweet wildfire that swept through her senses. Her untaught caress, at first clumsy and hesitant, gained confidence. And urgency was rising in them both now, and she found that she was breathing in fast pants, her whole body trembling uncontrollably; her passion was serious now, a pleasure-pain that almost frightened her.

'Don't,' she pleaded in a whisper as he bent to kiss her again. 'Brendan, please——'

He kissed her throat tenderly, then the soft skin of her collarbone, gently easing the fold of her dress aside. 'No,' she begged, as his mouth moved tenderly over the sensitive skin of her breast; she was aching for his touch, burning for it—and yet she knew it wasn't right, that she should stop him—

As his mouth reached the sweet ache of her nipple, she cried out aloud, cradling his dark head in her arms, and pushed him away, drooping her head so that her golden hair fell in a curtain over her face. She knew that she must stop him now, or else she would be lost for ever, swept away like a sail in the hurricane of his desire.

He stared at her with grey eyes that seemed to

understand everything, and although she could feel the strength of his need for her, he banked the furnace down with steel self-control.

'Thursday,' he said gently, stroking her trembling shoulders, 'relax, darling.' He took her in his arms, soothing her, calming the shaking in her body. But he could not satisfy the almost unbearable ache he had started inside her, and she was aware of wanting him almost to the point of sickness. Her head lolled against him—she was suddenly exhausted, and in the mood to cry bitterly. As if sensing her mood exactly, he picked her up in his arms, and as she clung to his neck, carried her down the companionway to her cabin.

In the soft darkness, he laid her on her bunk, and untied the belt of her dress.

'Please,' she whispered, but whether she was pleading for him to stay or go, she could not tell.

'Shhh,' he gentled her. 'I'm getting quite accustomed to undressing you!'

He slid the rustling silk off her hot body and laid the dress aside. 'I can't see you,' he said with a touch of his old dryness. 'Your modesty is quite safe.'

She lay against the cool sheets, helpless and shivery, her mind whirling in confusion. He kissed her with tenderness on each breast, then on her lips, and drew the sheet over her nakedness.

'You're tired to death,' he said softly. 'It's much too soon for any of this, isn't it? I'm sorry, girl. You're still weak. I should never——' He stopped himself, then kissed her softly on her brow.

She clung to him weakly, feeling terribly lost and dizzy, unwilling to let him go. But he prised her fingers away firmly and stood up.

'God, I've been a fool,' he muttered to himself. 'Sleep, Thursday. I'll see you in the morning.' He caressed her hair briefly. 'And thank you for a wonderful evening.'

'Brendan, I——'

But he had let himself out of the cabin door, leaving her confused and aching.

She wanted him so badly; and yet a part of her knew that he was right, that it was far too soon for any of this. His caresses had set her shaking like a leaf; she had responded to him with an intensity that had been almost violent. Why? Because it was all too new to her? Because it was too soon after her ordeal? Or were her feelings for Brendan becoming deeper than she imagined, deeper than she knew how to deal with?

From somewhere in the depths of her common sense she dredged the information that it would be natural—almost inevitable—for her to fall a little in love with the man who had saved her life, with whom she was cloistered in this tiny floating world. Especially if that man was as handsome, as powerful, as sexually virile as Brendan Kavanagh.

She was going to have to take care of herself—emotionally as well as physically. Brendan could be amazingly tender; but beneath his poised, calm exterior there lay a hard and dominating nature that could, she guessed, be utterly ruthless in pursuing an aim. He had shown good sense—as well as massive self-control—in stopping himself from going too far tonight.

And in her present confused state, it would have been very easy for him to have—

A shudder of mixed emotions passed through her, and she shut away the passionate images that rose, unbidden, to her mind. Brendan was not the sort of man to be played with. If she was going to commit herself to him, then she must do so seriously, with her eyes wide open. And if she was going to commit herself to him—whether emotionally or in any other way—she knew that it would have to be on his terms.

And didn't she have enough on her plate just trying to repair her faulty memory? Should she be even thinking of taking on the added emotional stress of an affair with a man whom she barely knew?

Yet she knew Brendan better than she knew any other human being in the world.

Better than she knew herself.

Suddenly, she was sick to death of trying to recall her past, of hunting down each clue, each faint chord in her mind. If it was going to come back, then back it would come. If not, well—

Sleep rose like a wave from the ocean depths, curling over her, and losing her in the velvety darkness.

A week later, *Seaspray* was within sight of the distant clouds which heralded Hawaii. The weather had been glorious, and the winds brisk enough to blow the trim yacht along at a steady pace.

The intoxicating evening days earlier had made them more awkward, rather than easier, with one another. It was extremely difficult to avoid someone on a thirty-six foot yacht on the ocean, but she and Brendan had been cool with one another, neither of them referring to what had happened—or caring to bridge the gap that had begun to appear between them.

In fact, their relationship had become strictly businesslike. She had learned an astonishing amount about the yacht and the way in which it was sailed. Brendan was a good teacher, and Thursday discovered that she was a quick and attentive learner. Once she had learned the sometimes confusing names of the parts of *Seaspray*, the rest was easy.

Surprisingly little attention was needed to keep the yacht racing along, and there had been oceans of time for Thursday to simply relax, lying cautiously in the sun, reading the books she found in the tiny bookcase over the chart-table, losing herself in the wonderful, peaceful rhythms of sailing life.

Dr Taveuni had been right. This was exactly what she needed to help her get over her ordeal, to set her mind at peace before she resumed her life. At first the mechanical effort of winching up sails and dealing with ropes had made her already strained muscles ache; but soon the pain faded, and she felt herself growing supple and fit again. So fit that she had begun to worry whether she wasn't becoming too muscular—but a glance in the mirror soon laid that fear to rest. Beneath her satiny skin, which was now tanned to a deep honey-gold around the fading pink blotches of sunburn, her sleek figure was attaining a feminine perfection which she knew instinctively to be right. She was not exactly plump, she realised, studying the almost angular lines of her hipbones, the flat plane of her stomach; but the fullness of her soft breasts more than made up for that.

More than once, over the past few days, she had felt Brendan's dark gaze on her, and had known, in some secret female way, that he was intrigued by her, that he desired her body. But although that thought made her heart trip faster, and sent a flicker of electricity along her veins, she had studiously resisted the temptation to look up and meet those grey eyes.

Now, as she and Brendan sat together in the cockpit and watched the misty white clouds on the horizon ahead, she was acutely aware of his presence next to her. It had been something of a strain to maintain the formal relationship between them—especially when the memory of his erotically intimate kisses, of the way he had stirred her profoundest feelings, lay between them, threatening to make her blush every time she met his gaze.

'It's going to be odd to touch dry land again,' she

said thoughtfully. 'I've got so used to the feeling of the sea underneath us that I'm not sure I'm going to like being steady again.'

'I know what you mean,' he smiled. 'But the longest stretch of the trip is yet to come—there's over two thousand miles of ocean between Hawaii and San Francisco.'

She glanced at his profile.

'Does it make you feel sad to think of parting with *Seaspray*?' she asked hesitantly. 'After all, she's your baby, isn't she?'

'Yes,' he agreed, smiling at her quietly, 'I suppose she is my baby.' He glanced up at the full-bellied sails above them. 'And it will be a wrench to part with her—now that I've sailed her this far. Maybe it would have been different if I'd just said goodbye to her in Australia. Still,' he grinned, 'the thought of sixty thousand pounds, cash down, does cheer me up a little!'

She gaped at him.

'Is that what she costs?' she asked in amazement. 'My God, I had no idea——'

'Sailing's an expensive business,' he shrugged. 'I'll be paying a hell of a lot more than that for *Whiplash*. *Whiplash* is a completely different boat altogether.'

'Is she bigger than *Seaspray*?' Thursday wanted to know.

'She's twice as long—with three or four times the canvas,' Brendan informed her calmly. '*Whiplash* belongs to a different age of sail. You'll know what I mean when you see her. She's not particularly easy to sail, though. I don't know if we'll manage her between the two of us. We may have to take on an extra crew member in the USA.'

'Oh,' she said, suddenly depressed at the thought of having to share this private world with anyone else. She had begun to get very used to having Brendan to herself—and the thought of another man on board was discomfiting. As if sensing her thoughts, Brendan smiled.

'You've quite taken to yachting, haven't you?'

'Very much so,' she admitted. 'Have you——' She hesitated. 'Have you got anyone in mind—I mean, to help crew *Whiplash*?'

'Yes,' he smiled. 'There is someone who wanted to come back to Australia on. *Whiplash*—though she hasn't quite made her mind up yet.'

'She?' echoed Thursday, an empty chill settling in her stomach.

'Marjorie Leppard,' he said, with an ironic glint in his eyes. 'She lives in San Francisco. Before I set sail in *Seaspray* she telephoned me—and mentioned that she had a vacation coming up soon.'

'Oh,' she said again, trying to shake off the gloom that his words had cast over her. She smiled brightly. 'Have you sailed with her before?'

'Oh, lots of times,' he confirmed casually. 'We once set off on a round-the-world trip together, in fact. Though we had to cancel that halfway through.'

'I see,' said Thursday, studying her slim brown hands studiously. 'An old friend, I presume?'

'Marjorie's an old friend, yes,' he confirmed. 'We've had a lot of fun together.'

'I see,' Thursday said primly, and he laughed at her tone.

'Don't tell me you're getting jealous?' he said, his face amused.

'Of course not,' she snapped quickly. 'I'm just curious. What does Marjorie do for a living?'

'She's articled to a lawyer's firm in San Francisco. She's a clever girl—she'll go far, especially with her looks and figure.' He grinned at her expression. 'She also happens to be a first-class sailor.'

'Lucky Marjorie,' Thursday remarked coldly. She didn't want Brendan to see how much his words had upset her, so she stood up hastily. 'I'll go and make lunch.'

She was half-way down the short companionway when she heard Brendan call her name. She came up again, to find him standing up in the cockpit, looking out to sea with a hand shading his eyes.

'Look!'

She followed his pointing finger to an apparently empty stretch of sparkling blue sea. And then, to her amazement, five smooth grey backs suddenly arched out of the water, glistening in the sunlight.

'What are they?' she gasped, watching in fascination.

'Dolphins,' he grinned. 'Aren't they beautiful?'

The magnificent creatures were all about the yacht now, surging out of the water in rhythmical grace, their sinuous bodies as full of power and beauty as some troupe of Pacific acrobats—acrobats of the sea.

Mesmerised, Thursday leaned over the rail to watch their sport. Every now and then, one would leap high into the air, to land with a crash of white foam, leaving her with a glimpse of a friendly eye, an almost humanly smiling face.

'They're wonderful!' she shouted happily, as a group of six or seven came splashing up to the stern, almost like eager puppies at play. Almost without knowing it, she had grabbed Brendan's strong arm in both her hands, and was laughing up into his face with sparkling eyes and flashing teeth. He stared down at her for a second, a strange half-smile on his mouth.

'I'm glad you like them,' he said softly. 'I love them, too. I always have.'

Two big dolphins arching over the stern broke the spell that his grey eyes had cast over her, and she turned to watch them, her heart pounding. The expression in

Brendan's eyes had pierced her to the marrow, leaving her weak at the knees. As she stared with unseeing eyes at the surging, arching dolphins, it occurred to her that he, too, was a free creature of the sea—as beautiful and as untrammelled as these delightful mammals.

'Come on,' he laughed suddenly, jumping over the coach-roof to lower the mainsail, 'let's put out the sea-anchor and go for a swim. I haven't been in the water for days!'

She turned to face him in alarm.

'But what about the dolphins?'

'They won't harm us,' he assured her, reefing the tall sail. 'Dolphins love people, though heaven knows why.' He threw out the sea-anchor, adding two drogues to make sure, and suddenly *Seaspray* was motionless on the dancing water. Thursday glanced in dismay at the surging grey shapes in the water. They were astonishingly beautiful to watch from the deck of a yacht—but the thought of actually swimming among them made her feel distinctly uncomfortable! Brendan was already hauling off his shirt and the Bermuda shorts underneath which he was wearing his black Speedo.

'Come on,' he grinned. 'Maybe they'll come and play with us—I've had that happen once or twice before.'

'B-but—what about sharks?'

'There are never any sharks near dolphins,' he told her. 'Dolphins chase sharks away—they don't dare show their faces within miles of a school as big as this one. Which is another very good reason for taking advantage, and having a swim.' He pushed her firmly towards the companionway. 'Go and put your costume on,' he commanded firmly, and she obeyed, though feeling somewhat anxious. Down in her cabin, she took off the clothes she was wearing and pulled on the lilac bikini she had bought at Tom Kandavu's store. When she had chosen it, almost as an afterthought, she had never expected to actually use it to swim in. It was rather minuscule, and its thin straps did not even begin to cover the patches of sunburn which were still visible across her shoulders and the tops of her full breasts. Making her mind up with a shrug, though, she ran back up on deck. Brendan greeted her with a grin and a nod—then dived, in one fluid movement of his magnificent body, into the sea.

She hesitated on the warm deck, her instincts rebelling against going in amongst those alien creatures of the sea; but when Brendan's head broke surface, his dark hair sleeked back by water, and called to her, she threw her instincts to the winds—and jumped!

The water was cool and delicious, and it was a shock to see *Seaspray* floating at anchor behind her, and nothing but the immense ocean all around. Suddenly, a pair of warm arms encircled her from behind, and Brendan drew her into the haven of his broad chest. She clung to his forearms, treading water nervously, and looked around.

'Where are they?' she asked apprehensively.

'They'll be back,' he assured her. His embrace was infinitely comforting, and she found herself cradled in his arms. The swells were smooth and—she had to admit—extremely pleasant, buoying them up with the gentle motion of a parent rocking a child. And then, with a splash, the dolphins had returned.

Half terrified, and yet overjoyed, Thursday clung to Brendan as the dolphins came gambolling around them, their glistening backs surging out of the water in lively hoops. The deep blue water was so clear that she could see the big animals swimming underwater, the sinuous grace of their bodies, their friendly, amusing bottle-nosed faces.

'Look at those two,' Brendan said in her ear, pointing to a pair who were plunging in and out of the water in what looked like a marvellous, life-celebrating dance. She had seen dolphins leap like that in films of trained animals, but she had never suspected that they performed the same incredible tricks in the wild state—for the sheer joy of it!

'Those two look like mates,' he told her. 'Perhaps they're courting now—or maybe they're an old married couple. They mate for life,' he added softly. 'The way humans ought to.'

Suddenly Thursday yelped in alarm as a stream of bubbles washed against them from below, tickling her legs and stomach.

'What on earth is that?' she gasped. Brendan was laughing.

'They're blowing bubbles underneath us. They almost always do when there are people in the water above them. It's their idea of a joke, I suppose.'

He released her, and she trod water anxiously, looking downward at her own golden-tanned legs in the crystal-blue water. Sure enough, the sleek shape of a dolphin was visible in the water below, and the silvery trail of the bubbles he was blowing ascended in a mischievous line around her. Brendan's face was amused, his grey eyes as bright as diamonds.

'Don't look so solemn,' he mocked. 'Come on, I'll race you round the yacht!'

He took off in a smooth, powerful crawl, his brown shoulders cleaving the blue water with graceful efficiency. Realising that she was being left behind, Thursday set off after him in panic—and found her own arms and legs falling into the easy rhythm of a respectable breaststroke. Well, she thought, as she followed Brendan, that's something else I've learned about myself—I know how to swim!

They stayed in the water for a delicious hour, paddling and splashing one another joyously in the lee of the white yacht. The dolphins were continually present, sometimes nearer, sometimes farther out, carrying on their own antics in friendly imitation. None of the big grey mammals ventured too close to *Seaspray* or the two humans—perhaps, as Brendan said, because they had had unpleasant experiences with boats and people before. But that suited Thursday fine; despite Brendan's assurances, she didn't altogether trust them!

At last they hauled their dripping selves back on to *Seaspray*. The dolphins had disappeared for ten minutes or so, and Brendan guessed that by now they would be on their way.

'They're heading in the same direction as us,' he told her as they flopped down on to the hot deck to lie in the sun, 'north-east to America. We may even meet them again before we get to LA.'

'That would be great.'

She glanced at his supremely beautiful male body stretched out beside her, and tugged her narrow bikini into some kind of decency.

'Do you often do this?' she asked, stretching her body out luxuriously in the sun's warmth. 'Jump off your yacht in mid-Pacific, I mean, and go swimming among the dolphins?'

'Only when the mood's right,' he told her enigmatically. She was lying on her tummy, and he raised himself on one elbow to touch the silky pink skin where her sunburn had been.

'Your scars are fading completely,' he told her casually. 'I said they would.'

The touch of his fingers on her naked skin had brought the golden hairs on her arms to attention, and a slight tremor passed through her muscles.

'I'm glad to hear that,' she said neutrally. The wooden planking of the deck, planed to an almost sensuous smoothness by master craftsmen, was warm under her body, and the caress of the sun was easing her into a state of treacherous relaxation. She was acutely aware of Brendan next to her, the length and power of his body, and she knew that his grey eyes were studying her figure with calm attention.

'I loved that swim,' she said, still trying to steer the conversation to some unemotional ground.

'Your body is lovely,' he said quietly. 'It was made to swim, to dance. And to love.'

His caress had changed to a gentle, firm massage of her shoulders. His powerful fingers explored the delicate grace of her shoulderblades, easing the tense muscles into relaxation, moulding the gentle curves of her firm young body. The deep comfort that his hands brought her spread luxuriously through her body. She began to melt under his hands, sighing softly to herself as his expert hands massaged the springy muscles alongside her spine, the tense place in the small of her back.

'Where did you learn to do this?' she asked languorously, her thick lashes closed over her eyes.

'Don't be so full of questions,' he reproached her mildly. And she felt his lips caress the smooth skin between her shoulderblades. 'You're so beautiful, Thursday Hunter. As beautiful as a wild gull.'

Dreamily, her heart surged at his praise. She raised herself on her elbow to face him, and he smoothed her sleek wet hair away from her face.

Her satiny skin was still beaded with pearls of water, and as he bent forward to kiss her softly, they could taste the salt on one another's lips. She stared into his deep grey eyes, hypnotised, as he caressed her soft cheek with his hand—and then slid his fingers to the back of her neck, pulling her face to him hungrily.

His lips met no resistance, and a long shudder passed through her as his mouth tasted hers, at first salt, and then intensely sweet. His arms drew her slender body against the hard male contours of his own, and she felt herself beginning to drift in a sensual ecstasy. Her own hands slid along his arms, revelling in the hard muscles, and then reached around his neck, her fingers probing the taut power in his body.

Their mouths were locked in an intimate pact now, his kiss inflaming her, piercing her senses in a way that was only a prelude to a more erotic pleasure yet. He pulled her body harder against his with a soft groan. There was nothing between them except the modesty of their costumes, and she answered his kisses dizzily, intoxicated by the harsh caress of their skins, his velvet against her satin. She could feel his virile need for her surging against her slender body, and she was suddenly as weak as a kitten. Brendan laid her back, the weight of his body half covering hers, his kiss plummeting through her aroused senses until her body strained against him of its own accord, obeying an instinct too deep and strong to be denied.

She had never known anything as profound as this feeling, this passion which both exalted her and set her aflame. Hungrily, her fingers traced the sleek muscles of his broad back, caressing down to the taut slimness of his waist.

His lips broke away from hers to kiss her eyes, her temples, her dewy cheeks. His breath was hot on her ultra-sensitive skin, the touch of his tongue searing the erogenous skin of her neck, the soft hollow of her throat. She locked her hands in his hair, gasping as his mouth laid a track of fire from the soft corners of her jaw to the base of her throat, his lips brushing the fluttering pulses there.

'You're so beautiful,' he murmured, his lips pressed hungrily to her delicate collarbone, his nostrils inhaling the faint, sweet smell of her woman's skin, the secret perfume that clung to her despite the pearls of salt water. She gasped out his name, terrified of this unbelievably strong feeling inside her, and yet urging it to go on, to take her to the end, whatever that might be.

As his lips caressed the tender swell of her full breasts, his fingers eased the thin pink straps down over her shoulders. She tried to resist him, but her treacherous muscles denied her mind, and he eased the bikini top down over her breasts, exposing the creamy perfection of her body. She heard his deep groan of desire as his eyes devoured the voluptuous curves of her flesh, and her answering shudder drew him to her again. Her shudder became a long-drawn gasp as his mouth explored her breasts, his tongue probing their rosebud tips so that they hardened in his mouth, firming passionately against the shockingly intimate caress that became an almost unbearable pleasure, a pleasure-pain that tugged at her heart, making her curl up against him, drawing his head away from her breasts to press her mouth against his own.

Now it was his hands which explored her breasts as his kiss intoxicated her. The smell of his musky skin was in her nostrils, the power of his muscles against her, and she knew that she was lost, that she could no more resist what he was doing to her than she could have stopped herself from breathing. Their hearts were pounding in unison, their kisses becoming rough and fierce with awakened desire. She pressed herself against him deliriously, her nipples aching against the roughness of his chest, and gasped again as his hand moved to her abdomen, trailing fire from the taut curve of her stomach down to the fullness of her thighs, and then back again.

She wanted him now, yearned for him with all the passion that was in her heart, all the love in her trembling soul. There could be no holding back now, they both knew that. They had committed themselves to one another with a primeval, undeniable urgency that could no longer be controlled.

Her arms around his neck tightened as he rolled on to her, his weight almost unbearably sweet, his mouth demanding and hungry, his hands tugging away her bikini bottom.

'You're so wonderful,' he gasped, his voice deep and rough. 'I've wanted you for so long, darling, held myself back for so long——'

'Why?' she whispered fiercely, burying her face against the hot velvet of his neck-muscles. 'Why didn't you just take me when you wanted me——' She broke off on a gasp as she felt him move between her thighs, his desire thrusting against her. As he touched her, an immense starburst exploded inside her head, a flash of unbearably brilliant colour that flooded her entire body, illuminated her entire being. She did not know that her nails had suddenly clawed into Brendan's back, or that her body had locked into a rigid arch. All she knew was that something vast and terrifying was happening inside her.

It was as if a thick veil, which had been hiding the sun, had in a single second been torn in two; and the light that was so convulsively revealed was almost too dazzling to bear.

As her vision dissolved into racking sobs, she clung to Brendan desperately, as desperately as she had once clung to the mast of a catamaran, swinging loose in a vast green sea.

At last she knew. And in that dazzling second of knowledge, Thursday Hunter perished for ever. And she knew that her long dream of forgetfulness was over. Knew that her idyll on *Seaspray* had come to an end. Knew that she was not Thursday Hunter, but Ingrid Marchant, of Barnes, London. Suddenly, she had a past, a source . . .

'*Thursday!*' Brendan's face was tight with worry as he stared down at her. 'For God's sake, what's the matter? Have I hurt you?'

'No,' she sobbed, the tears spilling helplessly across her cheeks. How could he know that she was crying for *him*—crying because her new knowledge meant that she now had a home to go to; that there was a man she called Daddy, waiting for her there; that she now had a million reasons to leave Brendan Kavanagh. 'You haven't hurt me,' she sobbed, and he held her close, trying to still the trembling that siezed her body.

'Then for heaven's sake tell me what's wrong,' he pleaded, his cheek tight against her temple. 'Have you remembered something—about your past life?'

She nodded, trying to fight back her tears. Memories were flooding back into her mind like a dam whose walls had burst, a torrent of pictures and names and faces that overwhelmed her. She squeezed her eyes shut as he lifted her into a sitting position, holding her in his arms. When at last she had the courage to look up at him, his face was intent and sombre.

"How did it happen?' he asked quietly.

'I don't know,' she whispered. 'It was you ... when you held me like that ...'

She tailed off into a silence, lying against him, and they both sat without talking for a few long seconds. They were both aware that in a sense their relationship was going to have to begin all over again—was going to have to be reconsidered.

And that there wasn't going to be any time to start again.

Brendan did not press her to say anything, leaving her to come to terms with her discovery in her own time. And when he sensed that she wanted to talk, he fetched a blanket from the cabin and wrapped it round her shoulders. They walked slowly to the stern, and as they reached the rail he turned to face her with calm eyes.

'I was getting sick of the name Thursday, anyhow,' he said wryly. 'What are you really called?'

'Ingrid. My name's Ingrid Marchant, and I live in a place called Barnes, in London.' She took a deep breath, and whispered the name that had eluded her for so long, that was now so wonderfully familiar. 'Ingrid. Ingrid Marchant.'

'Ingrid Marchant,' he repeated slowly. 'I don't know that I'm going to get used to that.' The sea foamed quietly in the silence. Then he reached out and lifted the little silver T that hung at her neck.

'What does this stand for, then?' he asked, holding it up. A dagger of pain twisted in her heart, and she looked away.

'Tom,' she answered dully. 'Tom Maynard.'

'Who is he?'

'He's my fiancé.'

The words dropped heavily from her lips. A bleak grey light came into his eyes, and she ached for the relationship that was disintegrating around them.

'So. You have kissed a man before.'

'Oh, Brendan,' she pleaded, 'don't look at me like that! Until you gave me my memory back, I knew nothing, absolutely nothing!'

'Of course you didn't,' he said coolly, and shrugged. 'How could you have known?'

'Why are you talking like that?' she asked in pain. 'I'm not a stranger!'

'I'm afraid you are, now,' he said coldly. 'You're Ingrid Marchant of London. I only knew Thursday Hunter, the girl from the sea.'

'But I'm still me,' she said urgently, grasping his arms. 'I'm the same person inside—I just know who I am now, that's all——'

'You know as well as I do that this changes things completely,' he interrupted, shaking her hands away.

'I'd half hoped——' He broke off, biting his lip, then decided to say it. 'I'd half hoped you would never regain your memory, Thursday. Because I knew that once you got your memory back, things would change for ever.'

'Nothing's changed,' she protested fiercely, but he silenced her with a finger on her lips.

'Never mind all that now. We've got much more important things to consider. Like a family who'll be going mad about you by now.'

'Yes,' she nodded slowly. 'I must contact Daddy as soon as possible. But——'

'Daddy?' A wry smile crossed his face. 'I thought you had no parents?'

'I don't. Daddy is—oh, it's too difficult to explain,' she broke off, feeling the tears threatening to well up again.

'You could try,' he murmured.

'Brendan, I want to talk about us——'

'There is no us, Ingrid Marchant,' he said harshly. 'As far as I'm concerned, my duty is to get you back to your family as soon as possible. So can we keep our minds on that, please?' His eyes were hard. She stared up at the man who meant everything to her, who had given her back her memory, her past, her identity, and ached.

'All right,' she faltered. 'What do you want to know?'

'Where your father is, for one thing.'

'He's in London.'

'Our radio will reach him,' he nodded curtly. 'I'm going to try right now. Come on.' He turned, and strode across the deck to the companionway. She followed him down into the map-room, where he had already swung the big black radio out of its cabinet in the mahogany panelling.

She waited in silence as he adjusted the dials with

sure brown fingers. A steady crackle streamed out of the speaker, and he looked up at her with cool grey eyes.

'What's your father's name?' he asked, pencil poised over the pad. She took a deep breath.

'Rear-Admiral Sir Geoffrey Marchant,' she said.

His smile was almost a grimace of pain.

'So—I was right about your father being a Navy man?'

'Yes, you were right about that. Daddy was a hero at Narvik, during the war.'

'I have to have a number,' he said after a short pause.

'It's 7345791,' she said quietly. Brendan glanced at his watch.

'London time,' he informed her drily, 'is precisely five-thirty a.m. I hope Rear-Admiral Sir Geoffrey Marchant is an early riser.' He picked up the microphone, and called up the London ship-to-shore exchange, requesting the number she had given. She waited in an aching silence as the operator's voice answered him, her tiredness at the end of a long shift carrying clearly over the thousands of miles. They waited in silence, Brendan doodling absently on the pad. Then the operator's voice came on again.

'You're through,' she said. 'Goodbye.'

The irascible tones she knew so well grated out of the speaker.

'What the hell is all this about? Have you any idea what time it is?'

Brendan's eyes met hers with an ironic glint as he turned his attention to the radio-microphone.

'Sir Geoffrey?' he enquired in his deep voice.

'That's right—and who the deuce are you?'

'My name is Brendan Kavanagh,' he replied, unperturbed by the hostile, upper-crusty voice. 'Do you have a daughter called Ingrid? About twenty-two, blonde hair, green eyes?'

'Of course I have,' snapped back the Rear-Admiral's voice; but now there was a wary note in it. 'What's she done this time?'

Brendan's grey eyes rose to meet hers again, one dark eyebrow quirking sardonically.

'She's all right now, Sir Geoffrey,' he replied calmly. 'But she very nearly got herself killed—and she's been suffering from loss of memory for the past few weeks.'

'Loss of memory?' snorted the Rear-Admiral contemptuously. 'What preposterous nonsense! Where the deuce is she?'

'I'm calling you from a yacht moored off Hawaii,' Brendan replied. 'Your daughter has been crewing for me on a voyage from the Fiji Islands. I——'

'Hawaii? Fiji?' The Rear-Admiral's voice was stunned. 'Look, young man—is my daughter there?'

Silently, Brendan passed her the microphone. Ingrid Marchant took it in a shaky hand and pressed the button for 'Transmit'.

'Hullo,' she said in a small voice. 'Daddy?'

CHAPTER SIX

THERE was a long silence in the little map-room, as Ingrid waited for the recriminations to begin. Brendan pointed at her thumb.

'You've still got your thumb on the Transmit button,' he said drily. 'Your father can't get through.' Hastily, she released the button, and the Rear-Admiral's indignant tones burst through the speaker in mid-sentence.

'. . . and of all your escapades, Ingrid, this is the stupidest and most pointless! Why aren't you in Hong Kong?'

'I——'

But before she had time to reply, the Rear-Admiral was thundering on.

'What your mother would have said, I dread to think! I can't understand you, Ingrid. I can't understand you at all. I suppose you've never so much as seen your Aunt Mabel?'

'No, Daddy,' she confessed in a small voice.

'Then where the blue blazes have you been all this time?'

'I went straight on to Australia.'

'Australia? What the devil for? Really, child, sometimes I think you're just plain——' The Rear-Admiral broke off suddenly as something occurred to him; and when he spoke again, his voice was heavy with suspicion. 'Tell me the truth, Ingrid. Is that blasted man at the bottom of this?'

'It was my idea, Daddy,' she faltered, avoiding Brendan's eyes. 'Tom had nothing to do with it.'

'But you've been staying with him, haven't you? Answer me, damn it!'

'Yes,' she said quietly, 'I've been staying with Tom Maynard.'

There was a crackling silence.

'Then what's all this nonsense about Fiji?' demanded the Rear-Admiral. 'And who's this man Kavanagh?'

'I was washed out to sea from the beach,' she answered simply. 'Brendan rescued me.'

'Then why the hell are you in Hawaii?' exploded the voice. 'Oh, to hell with it,' he said suddenly, his voice weary and disgusted. 'I don't want to hear any more of your lies, Ingrid. We can thrash the whole thing out when you get back to London.'

'Daddy, please——'

'I'm not interested. Put that feller Kavanagh back on the line.'

Ingrid hesitated, her face white, for an instant; then silently passed the radio-microphone back to Brendan, who was watching her with throughtful eyes. He took the microphone in his big hand, and depressed the button.

'Sir Geoffrey?'

'Mr Kavanagh—I don't know who you are, sir, and I don't really think I want to know. You sound like a gentleman, anyhow. Now listen to me—I want you to put Ingrid on the first plane for London today. Can you do that?'

Brendan glanced up at Ingrid, who had turned away, and was gazing out of the window at the distant shape of Hawaii.

'I'll do it if she wants me to,' he said quietly. 'I certainly don't want to get involved in your family squabbles, Sir Geoffrey—but Thursday—er—Ingrid is a grown woman, and she's quite capable of making up her own mind.'

'Don't be impertinent, sir!' snapped the Rear-Admiral furiously. 'Put that girl on the first plane, I tell you—or I'll have you arrested for kidnap!'

Noting the dangerous glint in Brendan's eyes, Ingrid leaned forward hastily to speak into the microphone in Brendan's hand.

'I'm on my way, Daddy,' she said. 'I'll telephone you from the airport to tell you what flight I'm on.'

'And no tricks this time,' grated the Rear-Admiral. And the clatter of his replaced receiver was distinctly audible across the thousands of miles.

In the silence that followed, Ingrid avoided Brendan's eyes.

'I'm sorry about that,' she whispered, twisting her hands. 'I suppose you're thinking the worst of me now.'

'I don't know what to think of you,' he replied, and his voice was surprisingly gentle. 'But it doesn't matter, anyhow, does it? You're flying back home again in a few hours, and I very much doubt if I'll ever see you again.'

The thought of it sent waves of misery through her.

Brendan stood up, switching the big radio set off, and folded it back into its compartment.

'So,' she said, almost to herself, 'Dr Taveuni was right, after all. You did give me my memory back.'

'Maybe Dr Taveuni is a lot cleverer than I gave him credit for,' Brendan nodded. 'Although I doubt whether even he could have predicted the precise method employed.' A hot flush rose to her cheeks, and he smiled. 'Your memory arrived just in the nick of time to rescue your virtue, Miss Marchant.'

'Don't!' she pleaded, the thought of that shocking, explosive revelation making her weak to her very soul.

'Anyway,' he teased, 'this will make a very unusual article in *The Lancet*. I've no doubt that you and I are destined to enter the pages of medical history.' He looked at her downcast head, a frown of concern crossing his forehead, reached out to touch her shoulder, then stopped himself. 'I must say,' he commented wrily, 'you don't seem particularly pleased to have got your memory back, young lady.'

She looked up at him with miserable green eyes.

'Oh,' she said drily, 'I'm delighted.'

'Look,' Brendan sighed, 'I make it a rule never to pry into other people's lives—but why don't you try explaining all this to me? For instance—who exactly is Tom Maynard? And what's all this about Aunt Mabel in Hong Kong?'

'You're right,' she said unhappily. 'I guess I do owe you some kind of explanation. I'm beginning to wish I'd never got my memory back, though. I could have done perfectly well as Thursday Hunter for the rest of my life.'

'Why?' Brendan sat down beside her on the settee, and lay back, watching her with intelligent grey eyes. 'Don't you like being Ingrid Marchant?'

She grimaced wryly.

'I'm afraid that's not my real name either.'

'This is like a Chinese puzzle,' he commmented with a slight smile. 'Why don't you just start at the beginning?'

'In the beginning,' she sighed. 'In the beginning was a foolish woman called Joyce Wentworth.' She paused, remembering her mother's gentle blue eyes and gay smile. As if sensing that her mood was somehow sad, Brendan reached out, and gently massaged her neck. The contact made her shudder slightly, arching her neck against his soothing fingers, so that her heavy golden hair brushed against his wrist.

'Your mother?' he guessed quietly. She nodded.

'Yes. I don't remember her too well—she died when I was a child. She made what was called an unfortunate marriage.' Ingrid sighed, trying to concentrate on what

she was saying; Brendan's firm, gentle fingers on her
shoulders were both disturbing and soothing. 'Anyway,
my father was a bit of a scoundrel, I suppose. Mummy's
family disapproved of him from the start. He was a
con-man, to put it bluntly—but he had all a con-man's
charm and mischief. I was very sad when he died.'

'So Rear-Admiral Sir Geoffrey Marchant isn't your
real father?' Brendan prompted.

'No,' she confirmed with a sad smile. 'He was a
distant relation of my mother's. When my father died,
he and his wife adopted me. Properly, you know—with
all the trimmings. Daddy—that is, Geoffrey—wanted
me to give up my real father's name. He said that would
give me a better chance in life.' She turned round to
glance at Brendan, whose handsome face was thoughtful. 'Is this all very confusing?'

'Not at all,' he said. 'How old were you at the time?'

'Seven and half,' she said promptly.

'Hmm,' he mused. 'Not an easy age to swap families.'

'No,' she said wryly, 'I suppose it wasn't. Geoffrey
and Marcia were very kind, in their own way. They
disapproved of my real father like mad, of course. They
said that he was just a common adventurer, that he'd
seduced my mother for her money—and so on. My
family,' she added drily, 'thinks itself rather above the
common herd.'

'So it would seem,' smiled Brendan. 'I take it they
didn't say these things to your face?'

'Not quite,' she shrugged. 'But it was always there.
They wanted me to forget him as soon as possible. I
don't know,' she shrugged, 'I was too young to
remember anything really significant about either of my
parents. I suppose Daddy may have been as bad as they
painted him out to be. But I remember him as such a
funny, kind man—and I'm sure he really loved my
mother . . .'

'And I take it—from what the Rear Admiral was saying back there—that you haven't been exactly a model child to them?'

'Not exactly,' she agreed. 'Mummy and Daddy—that is, Geoffrey and Marcia—were quite a bit older than my own parents. They really tried to be a substitute, though. They insisted I call them Mummy and Daddy—they were very loving. But I was just plain naughty, I guess. We love each other, Daddy and I— but over the past few years, it's been difficult. Mummy died three years ago. And after that, I sort of went off the rails a bit. I left college, and just bummed around for a long time—and that made Daddy furious. He's a real Navy man, you know.'

'I could tell,' Brendan said drily.

'He's mad about discipline and order—he's never been able to understand my naughty side. He thinks it's just perversity. He insists I inherited it from my real father.' She glanced at him with sad green eyes. 'Do you think that's possible?'

'No,' Brendan said briefly. He stared at her, lost in thought, for a long time, then went through into the galley to make them a cup of coffee apiece. It was still dark on deck, but the aromatic wind off the land was warm, and they took their coffees up on to the deck to talk some more.

'What's all this about Hong Kong?' Brendan asked quietly, once they were sitting on deck under a waning, pearly moon. 'And who's Aunt Mabel? And who's Tom Maynard?'

Ingrid sipped from her coffee and sighed.

'They're all mixed up in the same story, I'm afraid,' she admitted. She was suddenly uncomfortable. This was one part of her life that she was reluctant to let Brendan know about, and she began hesitantly.

'I met Tom at college. I—well, he seemed to

understand about me, and why I was the way I was. We became friends—and then—well, something closer.'

'Lovers?' Brendan asked calmly—but suddenly she thought she could sense tension in the big body next to her.

'Not lovers,' she said. 'Tom wanted to—but I'm old-fashioned enough to want to wait until after I'm married.' Brendan merely grunted. She glanced at him, but he seemed to be preoccupied in his coffee. She took a deep breath, and continued, the memories rushing back into the void. It all seemed so natural now, this past of hers; it was hard to believe that she had ever lost it. And yet she had meant what she said earlier. She would almost have preferred to have remained Thursday Hunter all her life. With Brendan Kavanagh.

'Anyway, Tom didn't meet with Daddy's approval. Tom's a bit—well, he's different. At the time I met him, he was going through this Hell's Angel thing—all black leather and studs. He had this ancient motor-bike, and he didn't wash very much——' She paused, half smiling at the memory. Brendan grunted again.

'Not exactly the sort of clean-cut young man to please the Rear Admiral?' he ventured drily.

'No,' she said. 'Daddy hated him from the first. He said it was history repeating itself. He said that Tom was a no-good, just like my real father. And that I was falling for his anti-social image, just the way my mother did.'

'I see,' Brendan nodded, tossing the dregs of his coffee into the sea. 'And no doubt that only made you rush into Tom's arms all the more?'

'I suppose so,' she admitted, glancing at him thoughtfully. 'Anyway, the crisis came when Tom and I decided to get engaged. We didn't get a ring—Tom said it was too bourgeois.'

'And no doubt too expensive,' Brendan cut in expressionlessly.

'That too,' she smiled uneasily. 'He got me this chain instead.' She fingered the initial T at her neck, still feeling slightly uneasy. Tom wasn't coming out very well in her story—and she was desperately keen for Brendan to *understand*, to approve of Tom. To see Tom in the way she saw him. 'Anyhow, when we told Daddy, he blew his top. He said he'd cut me out of his life if I married Tom—and a lot of other things besides.' She shuddered. 'He's quite a sight in a rage!'

'I can imagine that,' Brendan said quietly. 'And how did Tom's parents react to all of this, may I ask?'

'They didn't care very much. They've never cared about him,' she said bitterly. 'They were divorced years back—Mrs Maynard remarried, and lives in Los Angeles now. Tom's father just wasn't interested, anyhow.'

'How old is Tom?'

'Twenty-five.' She hesitated. 'That's what he says, anyway.'

Brendan looked at her sharply, a grey light glinting in his eyes. 'What do you mean, "that's what he says"?'

'Well——' she hesitated again, 'I saw his passport before we left Britain—and it says he's thirty-one.' she shrugged. 'He's always been sensitive about his age.'

'Indeed,' murmured Brendan. Ingrid sighed inwardly. It was so hard to make people understand about Tom—how senstive he was, how easily hurt. Very few people would ever understand him.

'Tom's very gentle,' she said awkwardly. 'He's more sensitive than other people. He's got this compulsion to hide, to lie about his real self—it's a sort of self-protective device——' She stopped. Somehow it wasn't coming out right. 'He's different,' she said lamely.

'You don't need to defend him,' Brendan told her

softly. 'I'm not attacking him. I'm just waiting to hear how you ended up on Hunter Island—and why.'

'That's a long story,' she said. 'To cut it short—well, when we announced that we were engaged, Daddy nearly went crazy. When he couldn't persuade me to break it off, he decided to send me to Hong Kong. His sister lives there—Mabel Hawthorne. She's the wife of a government official there. He thought that would get Tom out of my system—a six-week holiday in Hong Kong.'

'I take it you evolved other plans?' Brendan prompted.

'It was Tom's idea,' she said proudly. 'We changed the ticket without Daddy knowing. Tom joined me on the plane—and instead of getting off at Hong Kong, we flew on to Sydney together.'

'Very ingenious,' Brendan commented. 'What about Aunt Mabel?'

'Tom cabled her, saying that I wasn't coming after all, as I had 'flu.' She glanced quickly at Brendan. 'I suppose you think that's very underhand?'

'Who paid for Tom's ticket?' he asked, not answering her question.

'I did,' she said, her face colouring slightly. 'Tom doesn't have any money.'

'He's not working?'

'He can't find the right job,' she snapped defensively. 'He's really brilliant—but people are prejudiced against him.'

'Poor Tom,' he said, a light touch of irony in his deep voice. 'So—you went to Australia instead. Whereabouts in Australia?'

'We ended up in a place called Sugarloaf Point,' she said, cradling her cold coffee-cup in her hands. 'It's really lovely——'

'I know the place,' he said. 'I suppose you stayed in one of the beach cottages there?'

'Yes. It was a bit of a ramshackle place—but it was bliss. We didn't have much money—we were living on baked beans most of the time—but we had a lot of fun together.' Sensing the unspoken question on Brendan's lips, she shook her head wearily. 'No—we didn't sleep together, if that's what you want to know,' she said acidly. 'In fact, that was the way the whole trouble started.'

'Go on.'

'It was one night—Tom had been drinking. He does sometimes—it's another of his defence mechanisms.'

'Sure it is.'

She glanced at him quickly. 'Tom can't help the way he is, Brendan,' she said defensively. 'But he was a bit of a pig. He was being silly—it was coming to the end of our holiday, and he was tense. He said—well—he wanted——'

'He wanted your body,' Brendan said crudely. 'I know the feeling. Go on.'

'In the end, I got furious. I just ran out of the door, and on to the beach. It was a beautiful night, I remember, but I was really upset. I was crying—hurt and angry at the same time. After walking for about half an hour, I found I'd reached the little marina. There was this catamaran that was slipping is moorings. At first I just wanted to tie it up securely—Daddy taught me how to sail when I was just a kid, and I knew how to hitch the lines and springs. And then——'

'Then the idea came to you. A moonlight sail.'

'Yes,' she nodded. 'It seemed such a perfect idea. I would have brought the catamaran back, of course. But the sea was so calm—and there was a long path of moonlight across the water. It just seemed to be beckoning me—I don't know how to explain it——'

'Any sailor would know the feeling,' he said gently. 'Why didn't you take the boat back, then?'

'I went too far,' she said simply. She shuddered suddenly, the horrible memories rushing back into her mind. 'It was such a mad thing to do—I didn't have a compass or anything. I just sailed away, not thinking about anything except Tom—and how cross I was with him. And then, when I looked back—I couldn't see the land any more. And it was getting rough. A wind had sprung up, and the stars and moon had disappeared behind heavy cloud.'

'Yes,' Brendan nodded. 'The storm brewed very suddenly. What did you do?'

'What could I do? I was terrified. Within an hour, the wind had picked up to gale force. There was no radio on the catamaran. There was hardly anything on it— the owners had obviously cleared it out for the season. All there was was some emergency rations—which saved my life in the storm. And there was still water in the tanks. Enough to keep me going.' She shuddered again, going cold at the thought of it. 'I've never seen the sea like that—it was terrible! It just went on and on and on. It seemed to last for years. I guess it was only about a week——' She broke off on a slight sob, and his strong arm was around her shoulders, comforting her silently. 'I—I thought I was going to die. In the end, the wind carried the storm jib away, and I was utterly helpless. There were a few flares in a locker, but I never got a chance to use them. I barely remember landing on the island. By then I suppose I was in the last stages of exhaustion. All I remember is stumbling ashore through the coral reefs. That's how I cut my legs and feet. And I remember lying on the sand, waiting to die——' She clung to Brendan, reliving the horror of it. She pressed her face into his chest, infinitely grateful for his male presence.

'Have a good cry,' he advised gently, and she did exactly that, letting all the tension seep out of her in bitter tears that scalded—and yet somehow healed.

When her sobbing had died away, Brendan brushed her hair gently.

'It's going to be difficult at first—calling you Ingrid. It's a lovely name, though.' He eased her upright. The sun was just above the horizon, and a pale ruby glow had suffused the sky. Brendan stared into her tear-filled eyes.

'There's something else to be considered, Ingrid Marchant. And that's friend Tom.'

'Tom?' she queried, brushing the tears off her cheeks with a touchingly childish gesture.

'Yes, Tom. You realise that he didn't even report you missing?'

She stared at him for a second. 'But—but he doesn't even know where I am——'

'He must have guessed that you'd gone for a sail—or a swim. Why didn't he report you missing when you didn't get back?'

'I don't know,' she said uneasily. 'Poor Tom—he'll be sick with worry——'

'Poor Tom?' His eyes were hard. 'I can think of a lot of adjectives, Ingrid—but *poor* isn't one of them.'

'You don't understand,' she said defensively. 'He'll have been scared to death. God, I hope he's all right——'

'You hope *he's* all right? He doesn't seem to have cared very much whether *you* were all right!'

'But—but if he'd said anything to anyone, he'd have been in terrible trouble——'

'Don't be a fool,' he said shortly. 'His trouble was nothing compared to yours. If he'd had the sense—or the guts—to report that you were missing to the coastguard at Sugarloaf, you'd have been spotted and picked up within hours—a day at most. He just left you to die!' His words slashed through her mind like a knife, and she shook her head angrily.

'That's a horrible thing to say, Brendan,' she retorted. 'Tom didn't know where I was——'

'Where else could you be except on the sea?' he asked bitterly. His eyes were seriously angry now, and she noticed that his knuckles were white with the pressure in his clenched fists. 'I know what I'd like to say to your precious Tom——'

'Yes,' she snapped, 'you'd like to beat the daylights out of him, wouldn't you? You big strong he-man,' she sneered, 'you're just like Daddy! You don't even try and understand what Tom must have gone through——'

'I know what *you* went through,' Brendan interrupted sharply, 'because Tom was too much of a coward to report your disappearance. Do you realise that as far as he's concerned, you've been missing for almost a month? And that he still hasn't even breathed a word about you?'

'He's probably terrified,' she said. 'He's—oh, my God!' She broke off, biting her knuckles. 'When he found that I was gone, Brendan—he may have—have committed suicide!'

'That's highly unlikely, if you don't mind me saying so,' he retorted. 'Tom's probably back in London by now—and has completely forgotten about you.'

'You bastard!' she hissed, tears starting to her eyes at the cruelty of his words.

'I'm not the bastard,' he replied steadily. 'And I just get very angry when I think of you battling it out in the South Pacific, with Tom Maynard sitting quiet as a mouse back on shore. You were his responsibility, Ingrid——'

'Oh, really?' she asked caustically. 'A few days ago you were telling me that none of us was responsible for anyone else in this life. It's a rotten world, you told me, and it's every man for himself. Well, didn't you?'

'I said that,' he nodded, his cold eyes boring into hers. 'And I believe it. We're not responsible for each other—until we actually *take* responsibility for another human being, by our own wills. And Tom took responsibility for you when he got engaged to you. And even more so when he persuaded you to come to Australia with him, all secret and unknown. You do realise that he was the only person who knew where you were?'

'We decided about Australia together,' she snapped. 'And I don't want to hear any more of your accusations against a man you've never met——'

'I hope for his sake I never do meet him,' Brendan said grimly. 'And I do have some slight right to criticise your precious Tom,' he reminded her. 'It was I who picked you up on Hunter—remember?'

'Big deal,' she retorted, unmollified.

'You seem not to take your own life very seriously,' he said grimly, lifting her chin with his hand so that he could stare into her eyes. 'Are you so keen to get yourself killed?'

'It's my life,' Ingrid retorted, sullenly, thrusting his hand away. She hated this situation suddenly—it reminded her so much of other scoldings, other criticisms of Tom—occasions when she had reacted just as she was doing now.

'It's your life, is it?' he asked sarcastically. 'I never thought to hear you say something as childish as that, Ingrid. Don't you realise that other people care about you, care what happens to you?'

'Yeah? Like who?' she taunted.

'Certainly not Tom Maynard,' he answered calmly, and she flushed. 'When I think about it, it makes my blood boil. Tom must have panicked at first—that's how I see it. And then he realised that once he'd admitted that he'd taken you off to Australia, he'd be in dire trouble with your father. But he reasoned to himself that no one knew where you were. Everyone thought you were in Hong Kong. And when at last the news broke that you weren't with Aunt Mabel at all, he wouldn't be implicated in any way.'

'That's a vicious lie——' she began, her voice trembling.

'Is it?' His face was hard and unyielding. 'Your beloved Tom knew that he'd just have to sit tight—not say a word to anyone—and he'd never be associated with your disappearance. It would just be one of life's little mysteries.'

'I don't want to hear any more,' she said blindly, standing up and walking over to the rail on trembling legs. 'You're just like Daddy.'

'Maybe Daddy has a bit more sense than you give him credit for,' Brendan rejoined sourly. 'Can you explain why Tom didn't alert the authorities to your disappearance then?'

'There has to be a reason,' she said, gulping down the sob of mingled anger and pain that had risen in her throat, and turning to face him with shining green eyes. 'How can you judge him like this, when he isn't even here to defend himself? There *must* be a reason——'

'It had better be a good one,' he rasped. 'Your sudden reappearance is likely to give your fiancé a rude shock, Ingrid Marchant. You'd better break the news to him gently—you don't want to wound his tender, sensitive nature!'

'I've had enough!' she gasped, her heart thudding. 'I thought you were different, but I was wrong. You're just like all the rest of them, aren't you? A sour old man!'

'And you're just like all the other kids of your age,' he retorted, 'blind and stupid!'

'How nice of you to say so,' she said bitterly.

'You don't think you've been very clever, do you?' he asked sarcastically. 'I wouldn't call your little escapade the behaviour of a mature adult—would you?'

'Who the hell are you to judge?' she demanded. 'You don't know anything about me!'

'I know enough about you to tell that you're a callous little bitch,' he said calmly.

'Damn you!' she muttered unsteadily. 'I wish you'd left me to die on Hunter Island!'

'You've said that before,' he answered tautly. 'Maybe you're not the only one who's going to wish that.'

'What do you mean?' she demanded angrily.

'I mean Tom Maynard,' he sneered, standing up and stretching. 'Your resurrection is going to be very embarrassing for him—or hadn't you worked that out yet? A lot of people are going to want to know why he didn't report your disappearance in time. He's going to be the villain of the piece. And no doubt,' he said, his words thrusting home like daggers, 'he's devoutly hoping that by now you're just bones on the ocean bottom!'

Ingrid strode over to him without thinking, and slapped him as hard as she could across the cheek. His grey eyes blazed up like furnaces for a second, and his hands took her shoulders with a vice-grip that frightened her. She stared up at him with frightened, defiant eyes as he controlled his temper, his powerful muscles trembling with the effort. Her blow had reddened his bronzed cheek slightly, but she knew that the insult to his pride was far more dangerous—for her—than any physical pain she had been able to inflict.

He let her go at last, his face wearing a look of disgust.

'We live and learn,' he said softly. 'So now I know what you're really like.' The scorn in his deep eyes was too much to bear, and she turned away. He let her go, shaking his head. 'I preferred Thursday Hunter,' he said, his voice hard and cutting. 'She was a bit of an idiot—but she was a nice kid. Ingrid Marchant's a little bitch.'

She flinched, as though his words had been a physical blow, and whipped round to face him.

'You arrogant pig,' she quavered, 'you seem to think you're some kind of superior being——'

'I don't think anything of the kind,' he snapped. 'But you've changed over the past few minutes, young lady. When you didn't have a memory, you were almost lovable. Now—now you're a nasty little girl, just like all the other drop-outs and no-hopers.'

'You bastard——' she sobbed, but he cut through her sentence.

'Save it for dear Daddy. I'm not interested. I was also an orphan, Ingrid—and I also had hard times. But I didn't run away from any of my problems. Not once.' He wiped his lower lip, and she saw with a sharp pang that her blow had cut his lips slightly against his sharp white teeth, leaving a trace of scarlet on his tongue. 'As for dear Tom—whatever or wherever he may be—you'd better wise up to him, girl. He left you to die—and that's a fact.' He reached out, and lifted the silver T scornfully in front of her face. 'I'd throw this to the fishes, if I were you.'

She snatched it out of his hand, her eyes blazing.

'Don't tell me what to do,' she gritted. 'I've had enough of that in my life!' She spun away, hating him. It was as though the friendship and intimacy of the past weeks had never been—as though the sun-filled days and moonlit nights aboard *Seaspray* were as surely forgotten as her own past life had been. She turned to face him. 'I wish I'd never set eyes on you,' she said with concentrated venom. 'I hate you!' Their eyes met, clashed for an instant of mutual dislike and anger, and then she turned away, scarcely noticing the brilliant orange sunset that was illuminating the sky with glory. 'I'm going down to pack,' she said, trying not to let him see her tears. 'I'd like to get going as soon as possible, if you don't mind.'

'I don't mind,' he answered coldly. 'I don't mind at all.'

During the night, *Seaspray* reached Hawaii, and Ingrid awoke out of troubled dreams to listen to Brendan up on the deck, mooring the yacht. The next morning dawned brilliant and clear, the fabled crest of Mauna Loa towering up into the blue skies above them.

It was a day of frantic activity. After her long dream of bliss aboard *Seaspray*, the harsh realities of the real world came like a dash of cold water. For one thing, if she was to travel back to England on an airliner, she was going to need a passport. That meant a visit to the British Consul at Pearl Harbor—and he was none too pleased to be disturbed on a Saturday morning, normally his time for a round of golf.

As she sat in the office, waiting while one of the secretaries checked out her identity by telephone to London, the irony of her situation struck home. After all those weeks of having no identity, she was now confronted with the necessities of proving who she was. She stared out of the window at the azure sky, wondering about it all. She had still not yet come to terms with being Ingrid Marchant, she knew that.

Yet she felt no different inside herself. The only difference was that she could now remember her real name when she wanted to. She was not a different human being. Or was she? With the return of her memory had also come the return of all her problems.

And she had lost Brendan. Brendan, who was at this moment trying to get her on to one of the crowded airliners leaving Pearl for London, had become hard, cold and callous towards her. For a few wonderful days she had been privileged enough to see behind his severe, hard façade, to see the real man inside. Now, all that seemed to be over. She sighed so heavily that the clerk looked up in surprise at her. She couldn't imagine why Brendan was being so hostile towards her.

It never occurred to her that he might be showing the effects of his fear of losing her.

'Here you are, Miss Marchant,' smiled the clerk, rising from his chair. 'The Consul has stamped your new passport. You'll have to hand your old one back as soon as possible, of course.'

'Thank you,' she nodded, slipping the little blue book into her pocket absently. Her identity. The proof that was needed to tell the world who she was.

'You must have had an amazing experience,' the young man was saying, his bespectacled face eager. But she wasn't interested in talking about herself any more, and she excused herself from his curiosity as politely as she could manage. The prospect of her homecoming was looming large and dark in her mind, and as she hurried out of the Consulate, she had to fight back the tears. She walked blindly through the thronged streets, the realisation dawning on her that she had been happier as Thursday Hunter than as Ingrid Marchant. As Thursday, she had been offered the chance of a new start. As Thursday, she had been offered the chance of love.

And now Thursday was no more. Ingrid was going home.

The day was a Sunday, and as it turned out, the airport was crowded with holidaymakers on their way back to

Europe and mainland U.S.A. There was no flight earlier than lunchtime, and Brendan had insisted on staying with her until then. Having checked her baggage through the airline desk, they walked moodily over to the soft-carpeted restaurant and ordered coffee and a snack.

Brendan's face was grim, clearly reflecting his mood; and Ingrid herself found that she was toying nervously with anything that came to hand, her eyes downcast and her face pale—exactly like some rebellious teenager, and not like the poised woman of twenty-two she had once imagined herself to be. Thursday Hunter was dead, and in her resentment and anger against Brendan, Ingrid found time to mourn the passing of her alter ego. For all the problems that she had faced, Thursday Hunter at least had no past, no personality to burden her. When she had remembered herself to be Ingrid Marchant, the adopted daughter of the Rear-Admiral, she had reinherited a gloomy weight of problems that depressed her unutterably. Catching Brendan glancing at the big diver's watch on his wrist, she favoured him with a sour smile.

'Don't worry—I'll be out of your life soon enough,' she told him. 'You can start forgetting me right away.'

'You've got a great line in flippant dialogue,' he said tautly. She looked into the deep grey eyes for an instant, then looked away, shrugging to cover her discomfiture

'Why do you have to be so high and mighty?' she asked bitterly. The soft voice of the announcer broke into the muted hum of the restaurant, and outside a big jet left the ground soundlessly, shimmering in the haze that had already begun to rise off the tarmac.

'Am I high and mighty?' he asked drily.

'Yes,' she said. 'You're the most arrogant, domineering man I've ever met.'

'I suppose if you're used to weaklings like Tom Maynard, then I might seem that way to you,' he said silkily. She opened her mouth to retort angrily, but he held up a big hand quickly. 'Okay, no more about dear Tom—I promise.' She shut her mouth and looked away from his ironic smile, wishing she were already on the plane and far away.

'Only another hour to wait,' she said, looking at her watch—and felt a pang of misery tugging at her heart, though whether at the thought of leaving Hawaii or at the thought of going back to London, she was unable to tell. The waiter arrived with coffee and a toasted sandwich, and they ate in silence, watching the jets take off through the heavy plate-glass windows.

Brendan dropped his sandwich back on to the plate half-eaten. He grimaced.

'One thing I'm going to miss about you is your cooking,' he commented, brushing his fingers clean on the napkin. Ingrid looked up at him, trying to swallow her feelings of dislike for this big, handsome man.

'Will you—will you be all right without me?' she asked tentatively.

His mocking smile brought the blood to her cheeks.

'I'll just about manage,' he said with gentle sarcasm. 'You're not exactly indispensable.'

She looked away, effectively snubbed, and found that she was wringing her hands nervously. Angrily, she stopped herself—but Brendan had noticed.

'You're not exactly raring to go, are you?' he asked mildly. 'Is your stepfather going to give you hell?'

'I suppose so,' she said unwillingly. 'He's going to be furious, at any rate.'

'Don't you think he has some right to be?' Brendan enquired with one eyebrow lifted gently. She looked at him, noting for the thousandth time how magnificently built he was, how sternly beautiful his features were.

'Do me a favour,' she said nastily, 'and don't start lecturing me about the morals of it all. I'm going to be getting plenty of that at home.'

He shrugged. 'I'm not your father—thank God.'

'No, you're not,' she retorted. 'My father's dead.'

He looked at her intently. 'You're still wallowing in self-pity about it, aren't you?' he asked in a soft voice.

'What do you mean by that?' she rejoined in angry surprise.

'You think that because your parents died, the rest of the world owes you a living,' he said with a velvety, mocking smile.

'That's not true,' she snapped.

'Isn't it? You've been kicking against the world since you were seven and a half, Ingrid. You think that you're the only one in the world who's ever known any pain—and you don't ever intend to forgive the rest of humanity, do you?'

'That's a remarkably simplistic theory,' she said, trying to sound cool. But she was breathing fast, and her cheeks were burning with colour. 'I don't care to be psycho-analysed by amateurs, thank you.'

'You don't need psycho-analysis,' Brendan purred, his beautiful eyes glinting dangerously. 'What you need is a darn good hiding!'

'Oh, really,' she sneered, 'and I suppose you think you're the one who should give it to me?'

'Maybe,' he answered with a smile that turned her stomach over. 'Don't underestimate me, Ingrid— because I've half a mind to give you the spanking you deserve right here and now!'

The retort froze in her throat as she looked into his eyes, and realised with a jolt that Brendan Kavanagh was quite capable of doing exactly as he threatened! She shut her mouth hastily and buried her nose in her coffee-cup.

'Think about what I've said,' he pursued, more kindly. 'Maybe the reason you've never got along with your stepfather is that you're still resentful about your parents' death. And because your adopted parents didn't hide the fact that they despised your real father, and disapproved of your mother's marriage to him.' He smiled at her, his eyes suddenly sparkling. 'I wish you could see your face right now,' he said. 'It's the face of a spoiled child, petulant and twisted.'

'Can you blame me?' she asked sarcastically.

'The only time you've ever been happy in your life was when you were Thursday Hunter,' he guessed. 'Because then you'd forgotten all your real and imagined grievances against the world—and could just get on with being the sweet, gentle woman you really are.'

His words shook her, and her mouth dropped open. Was that how he really saw her? Sweet and gentle? Before she had time to reply, he was standing up.

'They're calling your flight,' he announced, cocking an ear to the dulcet tones of the airport announcer. 'Best get going, Ingrid Marchant.'

She followed him sullenly into the big departures hall.

'Thanks for the free psycho-analysis,' she said acidly, desperately wanting to provoke him somehow before he left her life for ever.

'Pleasure,' he grinned. 'Look, Ingrid—you'll never set eyes on me again. I've got no reason to lie to you. Remember my advice—forget your parents. You've got your own life to make now. So go out and make it. And stop feeling resentful against the rest of humanity. And stop hanging around with deadbeats and lame ducks like your friend Tom!'

They had reached the sliding doors that led out on to the apron and the roar of the vast jumbo was already audible from the hot tarmac outside. A pair of smiling stewardesses were waiting to take her ticket, and she turned to Brendan angrily.

'Thanks for the advice,' she said coolly. 'And now I want to leave you with a little psycho-analysis of my own.' She took a deep breath, staring up into the smiling, splendid face above her. 'You, Brendan Kavanagh, are without doubt the most arrogant, selfish, conceited man it's been my misfortune to meet. Just because you've made a lot of money building yachts and things it doesn't mean that you've got the right to tell me what to do with my life. You go to hell, Brendan!'

She stalked angrily past him, satisfied that her shaft had landed home. But the hand that closed around her wrist was like steel, and she gasped as he hauled her back to face him.

His eyes were laughing as he looked down at her; and then he pulled her close, his arms shockingly strong round her, his mouth claiming hers with a ruthless passion she remembered all too well. Furious and embarrassed, she tried to struggle—but he was far too strong.

His kiss was oceans deep, a torrent of fire that plunged through her senses, suddenly making her acutely aware of the hard male body that he was pressing so tight against her soft curves.

The busy sounds of the airport faded suddenly, as though they had both plunged into deep, warm water. Her very bones seemed to melt as he kissed her, his lips exploring her own passion with an intimate authority that staggered her senses. She clung to his powerful neck, aware of nothing but the strength of his body, the solid force of his shoulders, the sweet torment of his kiss, the surge of his male desire against her body. And her own need for him swelled like a river in spate, battering down her defences, the petty irritations she had felt against him, sweeping her into an admission that this man was unique in her life—the only man she had ever met who could stir her, shake her, thrill her in this way.

She was trembling when at last he released her, and her emerald eyes were filling with tears. Brendan smiled gently at her, kissed once again, hard on the lips, and then turned her firmly around to face the exit.

'Goodbye, Thursday,' he said quietly—and pushed her towards the smiling stewardesses, who were watching the scene with a mixture of sympathy and amusement. Blindly, she let them clip her ticket and steer her out into the baking heat of the airport apron.

The jumbo gleamed in the sunshine, a silver mountain, seemingly incapable of heaving its great bulk into the air. She walked on, not turning back until she had reached the very foot of the aluminium staircase that led up into the body of the plane. An unsteady crocodile of other passengers was following her. And in the doorway of the airport building, Brendan Kavanagh waved to her once, briefly, before turning away, and disappearing into the crowds within.

CHAPTER SEVEN

How strange it was to wake up in her own bed, on solid ground!

And how strange it was not to feel the rocking of *Seaspray*'s decks beneath her, the warmth of Pacific sunshine. Ingrid buried her face in the pillows, wishing she could go back to sleep—and resume the confused, delicious dream she had been enjoying about Brendan Kavanagh.

She had been in London for almost a week now, and it had been raining solidly the whole time, as if to match her own inner gloom. She lay still, listening absently to the sound of the rain on the windowpane, and of Mrs Johnson, the housekeeper, getting breakfast ready in the dining-room. For the thousandth time since she had left Hawaii, her thoughts returned to Brendan, and to the memory of that last, scaring kiss goodbye—a memory that even now made her stir restlessly.

Her homecoming had been memorable. Daddy had met her at the airport, grim and furious. He had been angrier than usual this time, because she had not only—as usual—disobeyed his wishes, but had deliberately set out to deceive him. And Daddy had a very harsh tongue sometimes, and a line of invective that had been perfected over years on the decks of battleships.

At first he had refused to believe her tale of shipwreck and amnesia; but as it became clear that she was telling the truth, his ruddy face had paled, and he had embraced her silently, his anger forgotten. But, like Brendan, he had known no words bad enough for Tom Maynard.

'By God, if I ever get my hands on him——' he had threatened darkly. 'Well, I hope this shows you, once and for all, what sort of man he is!' And he had bundled her off to see the family doctor, who had raised his white eyebrows in amazement at her story, but had declared her perfectly fit. The marks of her ordeal were almost gone now, anyway; even the sunburn, the pink blotches she had so loathed, had faded into the honey-gold of her skin, and only a few pearly scars here and there in the satiny perfection of her body remained as witness to her ordeal.

Yet she could not even summon up the enthusiasm to be grateful for this mercy. The threat of disfigurement, which had loomed so large in her mind once, had faded as completely as her scars.

She had steadfastly refused to think about Tom. She didn't want to probe either her own feelings about him, or his motives for not sending out search-parties after her. There would be time, later on, to deal with Tom. The past week had been spent in tying up the loose ends of her adventure. First of all, there had been the telephone call to an astounded Aunt Mabel to apologise for her deception. And then she had arranged a bank draft to cover her debts to Tom Kandavu and Dr Taveuni. She had written a long, slightly tearful letter to the little Fijian doctor, trying to explain who she was, and what had become of her, and posted it in a fine drizzle, thinking ruefully of Fijian sun.

Then there had been the business of reimbursing the owners of the red catamaran, who, it turned out, hadn't even realised yet that their boat was missing.

Her father had been very pressing about Brendan Kavanagh.

'I'm sorry I was so short with the feller,' he said apologetically. 'I thought he was another of your accomplices, you see. I wish I could thank him properly.' But she had been unable to say where Brendan was. All she knew was that he would be picking up his schooner around now—and would be sailing back to Australia. With Marjorie Leppard for crew.

Why should she care, anyway? She hated him. He had been crueller and ruder to her than any man she had ever known. He had said things to her that were unforgivable. So why was she still preoccupied with him? Damn him! It must be just pure sex, she reasoned. After all, he had aroused her with an expertise that had taken her utterly by surprise. She had never felt anything like that when Tom had kissed her. So it was natural that she should think of him now and then. But it was nothing deeper than that. And that was certain! Brendan was a hard, callous man, and better off left alone. Marjorie Whatsername was welcome to him.

And yet—and yet there was another part of her mind which knew that her resentment against Brendan was in part a side-effect of the problems she was facing in joining up the tear in her life. It wasn't easy becoming herself again; and every now and then Thursday Hunter was jostling with Ingrid Marchant inside her.

Thursday Hunter, for example, adored Brendan with the simple, pure passion of true first love.

Ingrid Marchant, sulky, difficult Ingrid, resented Brendan's calm maturity, his male strength. There was little doubt about it, she thought; her encounter with Brendan Kavanagh was forcing her, against her will, to come to terms with herself. Her loss of memory had been a wonderful opportunity to literally get out of herself, take a long, hard look at what she was doing and where she was going. Thank God she had met Brendan, and thank God that he had agreed to take charge of her for those weeks on *Seaspray*. No other man could have been so reassuring, so patient, so—she was almost going to say *loving*. And the things he had said to her at the airport, cruel and biting though they had seemed, had been true. Unfortunately.

Might Brendan be the vital catalyst needed to make her come to terms with herself? Might he be infinitely more than that?

Her bitter dislike of him was bound to pass. Ingrid Marchant was too clever a person not to know that it resulted from her recognition that his criticisms had been true—piercingly true. And when it did pass—would she find herself changing, perhaps for ever? And find herself, perhaps, in love with Brendan Kavanagh? Ingrid Marchant was in a state of flux, growing, though she hardly knew it, from adolescence into full womanhood. And the man responsible was thousands of miles away, sailing the trade winds on the wide wings of his boat.

But the thought of Brendan alone on board with another woman sent a sharp jab of jealousy through her, and she threw off the bedclothes impatiently, and stuck her grumpy self under a hot shower.

Sir Geoffrey, though retired for some years, still worked occasionally for the Admiralty, and after breakfast this morning, he set off for Greenwich, leaving Ingrid alone in the house.

It was, she had always thought, a beautiful old house, airy and spacious, with high Georgian ceilings and beautiful mouldings along the cornices. Its rooms were elegant, though very formally so, filled with antiques and lined with her stepfather's extensive collection of books.

It was also a slightly sombre house, and on this dripping, grey morning, she found herself restless and depressed. Perhaps, she thought bleakly, it was time to find out what had happened to Tom.

She had long since given up any pretence that she loved him. Although she had felt very close to him over the months they had been going out, she felt quite different now. She felt older, calmer. And less inclined to sympathise, either with her own woes, or with Tom Maynard. She had, after all, been making excuses for him for a long time—and it was true that he had behaved very strangely in not reporting that she was missing. She had a shrewd idea that he would be back in London by now—and suddenly, she wanted to see him, to find out what he was doing—and just what she felt about him.

She hesitated about just walking into his flat in Bayswater without warning—he might, after all, get a severe shock. But there was no telephone there—and as she headed towards Tom's place in a misty drizzle, she allowed herself one spurt of indignation. Hadn't he left her to die? Well then, he could stand the shock of seeing her alive again!

Tom's bike was in its usual place in the somewhat sordid little mews, and as she walked up the creaking stairs to his flat, she could hear the sound of his record-player. So—he *was* back. Deep inside, she had been secretly hoping that he wouldn't be—that he would still be in Australia, mourning her, or searching for her, Gritting her teeth, she knocked firmly on the door.

And she felt a moment of pity for him as he opened the door, dressed only in jeans, his thin torso naked. As he took her in, the colour drained out of his normally pale face, and he stepped backwards with a gasp of horror.

'*Ingrid!*'

'Hullo, Tom,' she said quietly. 'Can I come in?'

'God!' he breathed, looking her up and down, 'you nearly gave me a heart attack!' He paused, his brown eyes still wide with shock. 'It *is* you—isn't it?'

'It's me all right,' she smiled, feeling sorry for him as she noticed how he was shaking. 'Can I come in?' He glanced quickly over her shoulder, then nodded uncertainly.

'Yeah—of course,' he said, trying to force a smile to his bloodless lips. 'Come in, come in.'

He flinched away as she passed him, still watching her with wide eyes. The flat was in its usual state of disorder and mess; only now it seemed squalid to her, rather than romantic.

'Hell's teeth, Ingy,' he said, closing the door and following her to the dusty settee, 'I'd given you up for dead. What the hell happened to you?'

'I went for a sail,' she said simply. 'Why didn't you send out a search party, Tom?'

'A search party?' he repeated, beginning to recover the cocky composure she knew of old. 'They would have stuck me in jail for kidnap, girl! You went for a sail? So that was it. I thought something like that must have happened. And then, when the storm blew up, I thought you were a goner for sure.' He tried another smile, and was more successful this time. 'Hey, it's fantastic to see you——'

'Did you really think I was dead?' she asked quietly.

'Of course I did,' he shrugged. 'If I'd had the slightest suspicion you were still alive, I'd have called out the coastguard. But I thought you'd gone for a swim and drowned or something. And when you didn't come back—well——'

'You thought there was no point in getting yourself into a lot of hot water about a corpse?' she suggested drily.

'Something like that,' he nodded uncomfortably. 'You understand, don't you? But look, it's great to have you back——' He glanced nervously at the bedroom door, which was closed, and lowered his voice for some reason. 'What happened to you? You didn't sail back to Britain singlehanded, did you? And where did you get a boat from?'

'I stole one of the catamarans from the marina,' she said.

'Really?' he grinned. 'Terrific! Where did you go to? Weren't you caught in the storm?'

'Yes,' she said grimly, 'I was caught in the storm. I was washed nearly twelve hundred miles out to sea, Tom, and ended up shipwrecked on a place called Hunter Island.'

'No kidding?' he gaped. 'That's heavy, Ingy! It's a miracle you survived at all!'

'It was certainly no thanks to you,' she commented cruelly.

'Hey,' he protested, raising both hands, 'don't start blaming me for what happened to you, girl—*you* stole the boat, not me! And I didn't make you sail off into the sunset, did I? It was your own fault——'

'Of course it was,' she said wearily, suddenly not wanting to hear his excuses. 'I'm not accusing you, Tom. Only—well, we were engaged once. Or had you forgotten?'

He glanced uneasily at the bedroom door again, and then smiled at her uncertainly.

'Yeah, of course—we were engaged. So what?'

Ingrid stared at him, trying to see in this unshaven, half-naked lout any trace of the romantic rebel she had once wanted to marry.

'So—I just wanted to find out what had happened to you, that's all.' She studied him, noting for the first time how dirty he looked, how lined his thin face was. As if aware of her eyes, he pulled a grubby T-shirt over his torso, looking vaguely guilty, and shrugged.

'I waited for you to come back,' he told her. 'By morning I realised that something must have gone wrong. So I took a look along the beach, asked a few people if they'd seen you. By next day—well——' he shrugged again, 'I guessed that wherever you were, you weren't coming back.'

'Is that all?' she asked, nettled by his calm attitude.

'What else could I do?' he asked petulantly. 'If I'd reported it to the police, they would have started asking all sorts of questions. They might even have tried to pin a murder rap on me, who knows?'

Ingrid surveyed him with troubled green eyes.

'Weren't you even disturbed about it?' she demanded.

'Of course I was,' he said indignantly. 'I was really upset! I thought you were dead or something, didn't I? I just about cried my eyes out——'

The bedroom door opened, interrupting this sentence, and a dishevelled blonde with a sleepy face peered out.

'Tommy?' Her bleary eyes lit on Ingrid, and she smiled vaguely. 'Oh, hi—I didn't know you had company.' The painful silence that followed didn't seem to affect her, and she padded out, folding a greyish negligee around her ample body, and favoured Ingrid with a loose smile.

'Hi—I'm Patty. Tom's girl-friend,' she explained. Since she was very obviously naked under her negligee, her last statement was superfluous. Ingrid took the hand that was offered, and shook it gravely.

'Hullo, Patty,' she said quietly. 'I'm Ingrid Marchant. Just an old friend of Tom's.'

Tom was suddenly very red and hot, and he stood up, looking flustered, running his hand through his untidy hair.

'Well, girls,' he said brightly, 'what about a cup of tea? Or a beer?'

'No, thanks,' said Ingrid, feeling cold and somehow used inside. 'I just dropped in to say hullo. I'll be getting along now, if you don't mind. Nice to have met you, Patty.'

'Nice to have met *you*,' the other girl said. She looked vaguely puzzled, but was evidently intent on being amiable. 'Do drop in again—any friend of Tom's is a friend of mine.'

'Thank you,' Ingrid smiled gently. Tom walked her to the door, looking painfully embarrassed.

'Look,' he began in a low voice at the door, 'I didn't mean——'

'Please,' she interrupted him quietly, 'don't bother, Tom. It was nice seeing you again. Goodbye.'

He watched her silently as she walked swiftly down the stairs and out into the street.

Over dinner that evening, Ingrid was subdued. Her realisation of Tom's betrayal had not so much surprised as depressed her. As she had walked away from the dingy little mews, she had found herself wondering how she could ever have thought Tom to be anything other than what he was—a weak, corrupt, foolish person. So—he had been so concerned about her disappearance that he had taken a new girl-friend within weeks. Or had it been days?

Her sigh made her stepfather look up at her over the silver and crystal that decked the snowy linen on the dining-room table.

'Has something upset you, my dear?' he asked gently, surveying the golden sheen of her downcast head with concern.

'Not really,' she smiled wanly. 'I'm all right, Daddy—just a bit tired.'

She toyed listlessly with her food, and the Rear-Admiral filled her glass with red wine, his lined eyes still thoughtful.

'Look, Ingrid,' he said gently, 'I know I was very

harsh with you when you got back—and I said some things I shouldn't have——'

'It's all right, Daddy,' she interrupted, 'I understand.'

'I'm a crusty old sea-dog sometimes, and I know you think me an old autocrat. But it was all rather a shock to me. I'd thought you safe in Hong Kong, you see, and to be informed, out of the blue, that you were in Hawaii—well, it took the wind out of my sails——'

'Don't say any more,' she smiled. 'You were perfectly right in all the things you said. I'm not resentful about them.'

'I said them because I love you,' the elderly man said softly, patting her hand. His eyes drifted involuntarily to the photograph of his wife that stood on the sideboard. 'I wish Marcia had been here—she always knew what to do. As for me——' He smiled tiredly, 'an old man's not much good at trying to understand a young girl.'

'Oh, Daddy——'

'Just remember this,' he said quietly, still patting her hand, and looking into her eyes, which had begun to swim with tears, like wet emeralds, 'I feel towards you exactly like a father towards a daughter. And if ever you're in any trouble, Ingrid, no matter what it is, I wish you'd come to me.'

She nodded, gulping down tears.

'I think I will from now on,' she said a little tremulously.

'Good,' he nodded with a smile. 'Maybe we can start again now—eh?'

'Maybe,' she nodded, trying to answer his smile. 'I'd like to.'

They sat in the lounge after dinner. It was cold enough for a small fire in the grate—the autumn had come early, though it was only mid-September, and Ingrid closed the shutters, sealing herself and her stepfather into their cosy little world. Where was Brendan now? Sailing across the North Pacific in a stiff breeze? Basking in the sun on the deck of his new yacht? Making love to Marjorie Leppard? She tossed the thought aside furiously.

Her stepfather patted the cushion on the sofa next to him as she brought him his after-dinner glass of port, and they relaxed together.

'You've changed somehow, Ingrid,' he mused, staring into the flames.

'Have I?' she smiled. 'How?'

'Since you got back from your escapade, you're—oh, I'm not sure how to put it. Quieter. More poised. Altogether more mature.'

'I'm glad to hear that,' she observed gravely, passing him one of the Indian cheroots he enjoyed.

'Yes,' he nodded, watching her shrewdly through clouds of fragrant smoke. 'But you're also sad about something—I can see that.' He puffed thoughtfully. 'Maybe that's the result of your amnesia—I don't know. But I'm willing to bet that your rescuer—what was his name, Kavanagh?—well, I reckon he's got something to do with it. Had a bit of a crush on him, did you?' he enquired mildly.

'Of course not,' she said quickly. 'He was—he was—very rude to me.'

'Hmm,' reflected the Rear-Admiral. 'Told you a few home truths, then, did he?' He waved aside what she was about to say. 'Anyway, I don't want to pry, Ingrid. Whatever he's done to you, it's had the effect of making you grow up a lot—and for that, I'm eternally grateful to him.' There was another pause, filled only with the rustling of the fire in the grate. Ingrid nursed the half-glass of port she had poured for herself, lost in thoughts of Brendan and *Seaspray*.

'Anyway,' sighed her stepfather at last, 'you're going

to have to decide where you go from here, my dear girl.'
He glanced at her shrewdly. 'The university term starts
next month, you know. With your brains, you could
easily get back into a degree course—if you wanted to.'

'No,' she said thoughtfully, shaking her golden head,
'I don't think so, Daddy. Not yet, anyway—maybe
later on, when I get the education bug again. At the
moment, I'd just be wasting my time at university.'

'An education's never a waste of time,' he observed
mildly. 'But it's up to you, of course. Do you want to
get a job, then?'

'I suppose that would be the best thing,' she agreed
with a little sigh. 'Only I'm not qualified for anything.
Perhaps I should get a part-time job somewhere—just
to bring a few pennies in while I make up my mind
what to do next?'

'Good idea,' he agreed. 'What about that place you
worked at before—the publishers. What was their
name?'

'Benotti's,' she said, recalling her work there with a
grimace. 'That was a terrible job—reading through
manuscripts. You've no idea the rubbish that some
people write! No, I couldn't face that again. Besides,
that was full-time work. I want something that'll give
me time to think. Maybe I should try for some short-
term project. You know—something with a definite end
in sight.'

'By Jove, I've got just the thing,' the Rear-Admiral
said, looking up with a grin. 'I was talking to Pelham
Wright only the other day—my old First Mate, you
know—and he was telling me that he wanted a bright
young person to help him. I wonder if he's filled the
post yet?'

'What was the job?' she asked, mildly interested.

'Oh, general dogsbody, I think. Pelham's one of the
organisers, you know.'

'Organisers?'

'Of the Southampton Boat Show.' He flicked ash off the end of his cheroot, and looked at her with bright blue eyes. 'You've always loved boats. And you'll enjoy working with Plum—he's a real old character.'

'It's an idea,' she said thoughtfully, 'if he'll have me, of course.'

'Oh, you'll adore the International Show,' he assured her. 'It's held in Mayflower Park—it's simply massive. And people come from every corner of the world to show their designs off.'

She looked at him quickly. 'Do they indeed?' she asked, her green eyes narrowed intently. 'From places like Australia?'

'Of course,' he nodded. 'No self-respecting designer or builder would miss it. It's one of the world's great pleasure-boat showcases. They come from as far afield as America and Japan to give their yachts a showing. It's where they pick up most of the year's orders.'

'Really?' she mused, her heart suddenly beating a little faster.

'Interested?' he enquired.

'Yes,' she said softly. 'I'm very interested indeed.'

'Splendid!' He glanced at his fob-watch. 'It's not too late—should I give old Plum a ring now?'

'Yes, please,' said Ingrid, trying not to show her excitement.

The Rear-Admiral took his portly body over to the telephone and dialled a number. She listened with a mixture of anxiety and anticipation.

'Hello, Plum? Geoff here. Fine, thanks, and you? Good, good. Listen, old chap—remember you were telling me at the Club that you needed a bright young thing to help you organise the Boat Show next month? Yes, well, Ingrid's just arrived back from—er—Hong Kong, and she's at a loose end. But she's clever and hard-working, Plum. Would you consider her for the job?' There was a pause, during which she toyed nervously with her glass. 'Really?' said her stepfather happily. 'Well, I'm delighted to hear that, my dear chap. Yes, yes—I'll send her along first thing in the morning, and you can talk things over. Oh yes, she's done quite a bit of yachting. Splendid! I appreciate this, Plum. Not at all, my dear man. Goodnight!'

He turned to her happily, noting her expression with satisfaction.

'He's delighted,' he told her, coming over to sit with her. 'Come to think of it, I haven't seen you smile so brightly in a long time.'

'It'll be something to do,' she shrugged, trying to sound nonchalant. 'Thanks, Daddy.'

'Don't thank me yet,' he warned her. 'You haven't landed the job yet. You'll be meeting Plum at his office tomorrow to discuss things. And—hey!' Impulsively, she had leaned over to hug him.

'Daddy,' she said happily, 'you're an old sea-dog—and I love you!'

For a few seconds she debated whether to tell her father the reason for her delight—the chance that Brendan Kavanagh might—just might—be among the international designers exhibiting at the show. And then she decided not to—there wasn't much point in saying anything until she had found out for certain whether or not Brendan would be there. The thought of seeing him again, though, filled her with happiness. She didn't bother to reflect on her own perversity, either; that she had been mentally cursing Brendan for the past week somehow didn't seem very relevant. All that mattered was a chance, no matter how remote, of seeing him again, of looking into those deep grey eyes and hearing his masculine voice in her ears again. So she said nothing to her father; but the evening that followed was one of the happiest they had known together for a long time.

Lying thoughtfully in her bed later on, Ingrid reflected on her father's words to her over the dinner-table. Yes, she *had* grown up a lot since she had left Heathrow for her secret rendezvous with Tom those weeks ago. She felt different now—calmer, more adult. As though Thursday Hunter and Ingrid Marchant had fused at last inside her. As though the last vestiges of her confused, bitter adolescence had sloughed off her with her sunburned skin, leaving her fresh in the flush of her new womanhood.

As though Brendan Kavanagh had forced her to grow up. His methods were sometimes harsh, and his hard, often abrasive manner left no room for sentiment; but he had taught her a great deal, despite her resistance to him. On *Seaspray*'s decks she had learned self-sufficiency, balance—a capacity to rely upon herself. As he had taught her how to sail the beautiful white yacht, he had also taught her, as if by proxy, a way to steer her own erratic life.

Being Thursday Hunter had been wonderful, now that she looked back on it. Brendan had been right—she had never been happier. For once she didn't have to wallow in self-pity about being an orphan. For once she wasn't the rebel, kicking out at a world she neither liked nor understood.

She had also learned a lot about men.

Those shuddering minutes in his arms had changed her inside, maybe for ever. It wasn't like losing your—what was the word, virtue? Well, it wasn't like that. But in a sense, she had become a woman in Brendan's arms. When he had kissed her, touched the silky skin of her body, made her gasp with passion, he had made her fully aware, for the first time, of her own womanhood.

And that was something which Tom's greedy, damp

kisses had never done. And she doubted whether any man living could have done for her what Brendan had done. Yes—he had helped her become a full woman.

And for that she could never forget him. She *must* see him again! Dear Lord, she prayed, let him come to Southampton; let him be there, and let me meet him again—just to apologise for my stupidity and rudeness. Just to touch his warm, velvet skin again, to share those vivid memories of Fiji, Canton Island, that crazy night in Hawaii.

She lay on her back, hands cradled behind her head, and stared into the dark with wide eyes. She recalled that shuddering moment of revelation in Brendan's arms, the moment when his touch had triggered off the hidden key to her locked memory . . .

And slowly it came to her that her long adolescence was over. The ordeal was completed. She had passed the test of fire through which every man and woman must pass, the rocky wilderness between childhood and maturity.

It was as though her experience as Thursday Hunter had shown her the way—as though Brendan had guided her to the secret door into womanhood. Maybe that was the key that had unlocked her memory—the erotic male touch that had proclaimed her every inch a woman. The touch that had unlocked her sexuality. The touch that, as long as she lived, she could never forget.

It was true; Thursday Hunter and Ingrid Marchant were indeed the same person—not a static, unmoving sculpture, but a living, moving human soul that changed and loved and reacted to its world! How privileged she had been to have been given the chance to see herself so clearly, like Aphrodite being born from the foam, a beautiful, joyful, Pacific Aphrodite.

She rolled over contentedly, feeling that she had reached some kind of decision, at least. At least she was no longer going to pretend she loathed Brendan—that was childish. She didn't loathe him at all. As to what exactly she *did* feel about him—well, time would tell. And she would know for sure if she ever saw him again.

When she saw him again.

'Plum' Wright was one of her father's oldest friends, a rather gnome-like, balding man with a perpetual smile on his mild features. He had been one of the organisers of the Southampton Boat Show for the past two or three years, and he was full of enthusiasm about the big event.

'There's masses of work to be done,' he warned her, as they shared a cup of tea in his little office. 'Your job—if you take it on, that is—will be one of the busiest you've ever undertaken. But I guarantee that it won't be dull!' He wagged a small forefinger at her. 'Nor will it be particularly well paid, Ingrid. And you'll have to enjoy yachts and yachtsmen to get along.'

'I'm sure I'll manage,' she smiled. 'I'm afraid I'm not a very good typist, Plum—but I'll give almost anything else a try!'

'Excellent,' he enthused. 'You'll be my personal secretary. That's a nice way of saying general dogsbody,' he smiled. 'We have to do a lot of travelling over the next weeks, getting all the entrants organised, and making sure that every last detail is sorted out before the Show begins. That means racing back and forth between London and Southampton three or four times a week, and spending the occasional night in Southampton. Will you be able to manage that?'

'Of course,' she nodded. 'When do I start?'

He looked up with twinkling eyes.

'You can start right now, if you're so eager.' He swept a great pile of newspapers and advertising copy off a steel desk, and plonked a green telephone on to it.

'That's your desk from now on,' he announced, and gave her a bulging document file. 'Look through those—they're lists of all the yachting and marine engineering magazines in the world. We've put ads in quite a few of them. Your first job is to get on to the advertising editors of all of them, and make sure that the ads will be coming out in this month's editions. Think you'll manage?'

Ingrid flipped through the heap of papers and invoices, and the light of battle glinted in her emerald eyes.

'I'll manage,' she nodded, and scooped up the receiver.

Plum Wright kept her busy for the rest of the morning, outlining the tasks that remained to be done, and advising her of the procedure involved. It wasn't until lunchtime that she was able to get around to asking him for information about what really interested her.

'Plum,' she asked casually, putting down the telephone, 'do you have a list of all the entrants to the show?'

'Good idea,' he said, fishing another file out of his own voluminous desk, and hauling out some papers. 'You'll need this list.' He passed it over to her. 'Those are all the people who'll be exhibiting this year. Some of them are bringing boats to be demonstrated or displayed; the ones marked "Marquee" are mostly marine equipment people—sails, masts, electronic gear, and so forth. It's quite easy to work out who's bringing what. Now—how about a sandwich and a cup of tea at the place across the street?'

Sitting wedged between Plum and one of his colleagues at the melamine table in the little coffee-house, Ingrid studied the list with a ball of anxiety in her stomach. She had no ears for their complicated talk of the forthcoming show; all she wanted to know was whether Brendan would be there or not.

And at last, just as she was beginning to despair, she found the relevant information:

BERTH 3: SEA PANTHER LTD, Sydney, Australia. Marine design and construction. Brendan Kavanagh. Will be exhibiting PANTHER 36, racer/cruiser. Pontoon 53.

She looked up with a grin of sheer delight. Her gamble had paid off! Brendan was coming to Southampton, after all!

CHAPTER EIGHT

THE next weeks were almost unbelievably busy. As the time left for preparation lessened, so the tempo increased, and the load of work which Ingrid dealt with each day seemed to get heavier and heavier. She had never worked harder in her life, and never at such an amazing variety of jobs. Plum Wright very soon found out that her fair hair and green-eyed beauty, combined with her grace and charm, made her an excellent Public Relations agent, and she spent a great deal of her time explaining the point of the Show to various people. She also took orders, helped to arrange refreshments for the five-day Show, sent cables, took messages, helped arrange Customs facilities for. dozens of exhibitors bringing boats and equipment, played a part in organising the publicity, acted as buffer between the organisers and the local officials—in short, worked herself to a standstill every day.

And at night, she would barely have the strength to chew a few mouthfuls of dinner before slipping gratefully into bed and sleeping like a log. The Rear-Admiral watched her progress with a concerned eye—yet it was evident that she absolutely thrived on this formidable routine.

The weeks of dealing with strangers had put a fine polish on her natural poise, and her self-confidence had increased considerably. Despite the killing hours she worked, she was becoming stronger and fitter daily; those days of hard exercise aboard *Seaspray* had laid the foundations for a new strength that was both physical and spiritual.

Ingrid Marchant had been a pale, rather sulky person, who had tended to shun the world. Now, she was a happy, bright-eyed young woman who attracted male glances wherever she went. Her stepfather watched the transformation with growing astonishment, and then with heartfelt gratitude. His rebellious young stepdaughter, it seemed, was growing up at last!

As for Ingrid herself, the thought of meeting Brendan again kept her going when she thought her strength would run out. She was conscious of a new happiness, vaguely conscious that she was more poised and balanced than ever before; but she had very little time to think about her own self. There was simply too much to do in preparation for the Show.

And each day that brought Brendan Kavanagh a little closer to her also saw the site at Mayflower Park growing nearer to completion. A special marina had been constructed on Southampton Water where dozens of exhibitors would have boats ready to be tried out or demonstrated. Overlooking this scene of frantic activity was the vast main exhibition area where the main bulk of the exhibits would be sited. Other boats would be displayed here, in the open air, so that prospective customers could take in the entire craft at a glance. Marquees would shelter other displays, all concerned with the mysteries of yachting, from diesel engines to electronic navigation sytems, from sails to foul weather clothing.

Almost everything connected with boats and yachting would be visible and available. There would be yachts of every kind, from trimarans to towering racers, and in every stage of construction, from empty hulls ready for backyard fitting-out to gleaming and expensive fully-completed cruisers.

Ingrid found it all fascinating, and what was more, deeply exciting. The sea was in her blood, and in the few minutes of spare time she could snatch from her schedule, she would sit back in her chair with a half-smile on her leaf-shaped mouth, dreaming of those sun-drenched days aboard *Seapsray*.

How was Brendan going to react to seeing her again? In her sweetest daydreams, she would see those grey eyes widen with pleasure as he saw her; he would throw his arms wide, and hug the breath out of her. Later, they would find themselves in a candlelit restaurant somewhere, talking in soft, intimate tones . . .

And being a practical woman, she stopped her fantasies firmly at that point. That was as far as she could go—to expect any more would be simply setting herself up for a disappointment.

The first exhibitors began to trickle in at last, setting up stands here and there in the empty marquees. Southampton was responding with a constant fine drizzle, and the sweep of the exhibition park began to be dotted with raincoated and umbrellaed figures carrying reels of flex to and fro.

From now on, Ingrid had to be on hand more or less constantly, as she had been given the job of liaising between the exhibitors and Plum Wright.

'Just smooth any ruffled feathers, Ingrid, and make sure everyone's happy,' Plum had blithely requested—as though this would be the simplest task in the world.

The trickle suddenly became a flood. Yachts began to arrive, by sea and land, and even, in one case, by helicopter. The ground was thronged with trucks and lorries delivering, fetching, hooting, unloading; the once-empty marquees suddenly began to bustle with life as literally hundreds of stands sprang up out of nowhere.

The superb organisation and planning which had gone into the show now became apparent; each company had its own allotted stand or berth—some had used the same place for many years—and despite the hectic activity, there was very little confusion, and very few lost tempers.

Ingrid waited anxiously for Brendan's arrival. She had long since located the berth at the marina where his yacht was booked in, and she checked it eagerly when she arrived each morning, hoping that a tall white sail would be standing in the grey water there.

But while everyone else seemed to be arriving daily, there was no news yet from Sea Panther Ltd. When he had still not arrived, two days before the official opening, misery descended upon her. He wasn't coming! He had decided against Southampton this year—or hadn't had the time—or had damaged his display yacht—or (God forbid) had hurt himself. That Thursday she became restless and depressed, fretting and fussing over Brendan's non-appearance. Plum, who drove her home that night, put her unhappy mood down to overwork.

'In twenty-four hours the Show'll be under way,' he consoled her, 'and then you can sleep for a week!'

She smiled wanly. But the next morning, as Plum drove his old Rover through the crowds towards the Information marquee, Ingrid's heart jolted hard inside her. The tall masts of a yacht were visible against the pontoon where Brendan's company had been allocated a berth. As soon as Plum stopped the car, she jumped out breathlessly.

'I have to check something down at the Marina,' she told him hastily. 'I'll be back in a minute.'

'All right,' nodded Plum jovially, and she raced off nervously, pausing at the ladies' to check her make-up. He was here! She had had a feeling that he would arrive this morning, and as she tremblingly applied a touch of gloss to her lovely mouth, she was grateful that she had chosen to wear one of her favourite outfits, a dove-grey suit with a cream silk blouse. Studying herself in the mirror, she had a moment of dismay. She looked so severe! She had wanted to appear more feminine than that! Hastily, she undid another pearl button on the blouse, revealing a tantalising glimpse of the satiny skin of her upper breasts. That was a little better. Her golden hair, heavier and silkier now, and also more curly in England's damp air, fell in a gleaming cascade to her shoulders, and the Pacific tan had receded very slightly, revealing the dusky roses in her cheeks.

She looked right, she thought. The severe elegance of the French suit could not disguise the youthful femininity of her figure; and yet its sophistication helped emphasise her natural poise. The soft material of the jacket clung tantalisingly to the eager thrust of her taut breasts, flattering her slender waist, the full chalice of her hips.

With her heart in her mouth, she walked down through the crowds of technicians and exhibitors to Brendan's yacht. As she descended the stairs to the marina, she could see that the yacht was a good ten feet longer than *Seaspray*, and had been finished in a trim red and blue. The name painted on her stern was *Southern Cross*. Ingrid walked to the mooring, and paused uncertainly, looking down on to the finely-laid teak planking of the deck. There seemed to be no one in sight at first; and then she heard someone climbing up the companionway from below.

And Brendan climbed lithely over the coach-roof, his arms full of nylon cording. Ingrid thought her heart had stopped. She had forgotten quite how physically beautiful he was, so powerfully built and yet so graceful, his mahogany skin dark against the white cotton shirt which he wore.

He must have sensed, rather than heard, her slight gasp; he turned sharply to look at her, his deep grey eyes locking on hers in a way that jolted her so hard in the solar plexus that she felt suddenly giddy. For a spinning eternity they stared at one another; and then Brendan dropped the ropes he had been carrying, and walked slowly towards her, a slight smile creasing the corner of his mouth, one eyebrow raised in that ironic tilt which she knew so well. She began to breathe again, uncertainly, as he stepped across on to the jetty and came up to her, staring down at her from his authoritative height.

'Hullo, Ingrid Marchant,' he said in his deep, silky voice. There was no hug, no kiss of greeting. Biting back her nervous disappointment, she tried to sound cool in return.

'Hullo, Brendan,' she said softly. 'Welcome to Southampton.'

His eyes drifted up and down her figure, mockingly appreciative.

'Well, well,' he purred. 'You look very—different. The last time I saw you, you were a tearstained waif in a Polynesian skirt. Now——'

Uncertain whether he was teasing her or not, she flushed slightly.

'Did you get *Seaspray* to San Francisco okay?' she asked.

'Sure,' he shrugged, 'I made record time on the way back, too. I picked up *Whiplash*, and——' He paused, his eyes drawn to the name-tag that was pinned to her jacket. His eyebrows questioned her. 'Are you part of the Show?' he asked in surprise.

'Just a general dogsbody,' she smiled. Oh, it was good to see him again! She ached to throw herself into his arms, to kiss that firm, passionate mouth in the way she wanted to. This casual reunion wasn't what she had dreamed about at all——

'Quite a coincidence,' said Brendan with a touch of

irony in his voice. 'What on earth drew you to the Southampton Boat Show? Wait—don't tell me. Your daddy's a Rear-Admiral, isn't he?'

'Yes,' she nodded. 'As a matter of fact——' She hesitated, and he tilted his head on one side.

'What?'

'I took this job—well, on the offchance that you'd be—I mean, that I might see you——' She stopped in confusion, cursing herself. She hadn't meant to give him the impression that she was chasing after him. And the grim expression that had suddenly appeared in his eyes told her that she had blundered.

'On the offchance that I'd be coming?' He shook his head slightly. 'That was very stupid of you, Ingrid. There's absolutely nothing between us. It would have been better if you'd left well alone.'

She blushed furiously at his unexpected antagonism.

'I don't have any ulterior motives,' she told him crossly. 'I just wanted to see you again, to thank you for what you did for me——'

'No thanks are needed,' he interrupted calmly. His grey eyes seemed to be piercing her, penetrating into her very heart of hearts. And his expression was distinctly cold now. 'May I remind you that we didn't part on the best of terms,' he said austerely. 'You and I are chalk and cheese, Ingrid. Oil and water. We don't mix.'

'You're still not angry about our quarrel, are you?' she asked with wide green eyes. 'I wanted to apologise about that, Brendan. I was terribly rude to you, but——'

'Please,' he interrupted quietly, turning away. 'I'm a busy man, Ingrid. Can we cut this short?'

She stared at him in desolation and shock. He was clearly very angry now, his powerful arms taut and his jaw-muscles clenched. Oh, dear God, she groaned inwardly, did he really feel that strongly about her?

'Brendan,' she began in a whisper, 'don't be cruel like

this—I'm sorry for my rudeness. I've been longing to see you again——'

'Please,' he grated, 'no more sentimentality, Ingrid.' His cold eyes impaled her, and she realised with dismay that his face had gone pale and taut. It had not occurred to her in her wildest dreams that he would react like this towards her.

'But——' she shook her golden head helplessly, 'I've been dreaming of this for weeks—can't we make it up somehow——?'

'For God's sake,' he snarled, his big hands grasping her arms with steely anger, 'are you deaf? I don't want to see you again. Understand? I'm not interested!' He stared into her eyes passionately, his mouth a hard, grim line, then released her. 'Now leave me alone—I've only got a few hours to get this boat ready for the Show—and she's been at sea for well over a month.'

Ingrid stood, trembling with shock, as he turned away from her.

'Brendan——' she whispered, then stopped. Someone else had emerged from the companionway—a tall, dark-eyed brunette, whose voluptuous figure was emphasised by the tight sweater and jeans which she wore. She stepped out on to the deck in very un-sailorly high heels, and looked up at Ingrid's pale face with thinly-veiled hostility. Brendan smiled sourly at Ingrid.

'Ingrid—meet my crew, Marjorie Leppard. She helped sail *Southern Cross* to Southampton. Marje, this is Ingrid Marchant—otherwise known as Thursday Hunter.'

'So,' said Marjorie Leppard with a tense smile, '*you're* Thursday Hunter? I've heard such a lot about you.' She stepped up on to the jetty with the lithe grace of a cat, and took Brendan's arm possessively in both hands, nestling her body provocatively up to him. 'Delighted to meet you,' she purred. But her eyes sent Ingrid an unmistakable—and lethal—challenge.

Stunned, Ingrid felt her world falling apart around her ears. She looked from Marjorie Leppard's sultry, insolent smile to Brendan's cold eyes, and managed to stammer out some kind of a greeting. The other woman's red-nailed fingers caressed the mahogany strength of Brendan's arm with challenging eroticism, and Ingrid tried to bite back her bitter hurt and fury.

'Well,' she said, managing a tight little smile, 'I'd better get back to my work. I've got a lot to do. So long.' And turned on her heel blindly, walking back through the crowds to the Information marquee, her beautiful green eyes swimming with tears.

God, what a fool she had been! Fool, fool, fool! Had she really imagined that Brendan Kavanagh would be unattached and available? Feeling sobs dangerously close, Ingrid slipped back into the ladies'—and in that unglamorous refuge, tried to control her feelings.

A disappointment sharper than she had ever known was aching inside her. She pressed her palms to her eyes, trying to stop the tears from spilling out. It was over. Her sweet, sweet daydream was over for ever—it had simply crumbled away, as all daydreams are doomed to do.

'Ingrid?'

She raised her head vaguely to stare at her stepfather, whose blue eyes were watching her with deep concern.

'Oh. Sorry, Daddy—I was just dreaming.' She picked up her knife and fork listlessly, and pretended to eat some dinner. It had been a dreadful day. How she had managed to come through it she didn't know; it had been like some never-ending dream, and she had spent the day in a kind of daze, doing all that was required of her as if by remote-control, while her stunned mind looked on without participating.

'Is anything the matter, child?' The Rear-Admiral

rested the back of his fingers lightly against her forehead, testing her temperature. It was a gesture she remembered so well from her childhood, and now it made her smile at him despite her misery.

'I'm all right, Daddy. Just a bit tired.'

'Hmmm. I would have thought you'd be overjoyed, now that the Show's about to begin.' He looked at her enquiringly. 'Has it been a bit of an anticlimax, eh?'

An anticlimax? Not quite. You couldn't call the destruction of all your hopes an anticlimax. But she smiled wanly, not wanting to be questioned further, and nodded.

'I suppose so. I think I'll get an early night, if you don't mind, Daddy.' She pushed her untouched food away and made to stand up.

'Oh, don't go to bed yet,' the Rear-Admiral protested. 'Stay and have a whisky with me—you look as though you could do with a drink. In fact,' he added, as she sat unwillingly down again, 'you look about done in, Ingrid. Are you sure nothing's happened to upset you today?'

'Nothing, really. It's just been madly busy, that's all.'

She followed her stepfather dully through into the sitting-room, and accepted the glass of whisky he poured her with a slight smile. The medicinal bite of the golden liquid was heartening.

'So,' smiled her stepfather, sitting down beside her, 'tell me about your day. Has everyone arrived yet?'

'Yes—the last ones came in today.' She hesitated, longing to talk about Brendan, yet dreading to. 'Brendan Kavanagh arrived today,' she said at last. 'The man who picked me up off Hunter Island.'

'Good lord!' exclaimed the Rear-Admiral. 'Kavanagh? But, my dear child, why didn't you ask him to dinner? I absolutely *must* meet the man and thank him——'

'He seemed rather busy,' she said drily. 'He's got a lot of things to do.'

'But did you know he was coming to Southampton? Why didn't you say anything? We must have him round here for a meal—or for drinks, at the very least!'

'I've got a feeling he'll be much too busy for anything like that,' she said quietly, and he shot her a penetrating glance. 'I don't think we should ask him, Daddy.'

'But, Ingrid——' He stopped himself, watching her with intelligent, lined eyes as she gulped at her whisky. He seemed about to say something else, and then stopped again. 'Whatever you think best,' he said at last. 'I shan't intrude, of course.' But his face was thoughtful, and the eyes that rested on his daughter's tired face were shrewd and concerned. 'I shan't intrude,' he repeated gently.

She was almost too exhausted to go to work the next morning—but it was the first day of the Show, and she knew that Plum was going to depend on her. She hauled herself out of bed at the last possible moment, showered perfunctorily, and managed to gulp down a cup of black coffee before he arrived to pick her up in his old Rover.

Plum was full of excitement at the culmination of what had been more or less a full year's planning; but he was not too excited to notice that his young assistant was unusually quiet—or that there were dark smudges under normally crystal-clear eyes. But tact was one of Plum Wright's chief qualities, and after she had replied tersely to one or two of his gentle enquiries, he left her alone, and they drove to Southampton in silence. He glanced at her from time to time, his gnome-like face impassive, but she did not notice.

The day passed in a whirl of duties and tasks. The public had begun to flood into the huge park from the moment the gates opened, and Ingrid was besieged with exhibitors and officials needing her services in one way or another. She buried herself in her work, trying not to think about Brendan and Marjorie Leppard, simply grateful that there was something to occupy her sad thoughts with.

At around three-thirty in the afternoon, though, Plum took pity on her pale face and drooping eyelids.

'Jack Ford is going back to London in a few minutes,' he told her kindly. 'You go back home with him—you're tired out.' She opened her mouth to protest that she felt fine, but Plum was firm. 'Go to bed with a good book—that's my advice,' he smiled. 'Cocoa and rest—that's the ticket!'

Inwardly relieved to be leaving the hurly-burly a good few hours early, she nodded. 'Perhaps you're right, Plum. I'll get my coat.'

But as she walked wearily through the door of the tiny cubicle she used as an office, she was brought up short in front of a tall male figure. Brendan.

'Are you busy?' he asked without preliminaries.

'I was just about to leave,' she answered coolly, trying not to show him how much his appearance had disturbed her. 'Was there something you wanted?'

'I wanted a word with you, as a matter of fact,' he said.

She glared defiantly up at his masterful face.

'In my official capacity?'

'In your private capacity.'

'I'm sorry,' she announced coldly, 'my private capacity is just going home.'

'Sit down and don't be a fool,' he growled, propelling her backwards so that she was forced to sit with undignified haste on her own chair. He perched himself on her desk and stared down at her. 'I want to talk to you.'

'Someone's taking me back to London now——'

'I'm driving in myself in half an hour,' he said calmly. 'I'll take you in my car.'

'Oh?' she said, raising cool eyebrows. 'Has Marjorie let you off the leash tonight?'

The glint of anger in his eyes was quickly repressed.

'You might as well ride with me,' he told her. 'I'm going to your house, after all.'

'My house?' she gasped. 'What for?'

'You father asked me round for drinks.' He surveyed her with dispassionate eyes. 'You look worn out. Have you been working too hard?'

'When did Daddy ask you round for drinks?' she asked in amazement.

He smiled with a hint of irony.

'Lunchtime today. One of your colleagues called me to a telephone, and lo and behold . . . I take it you don't mind?'

'Why should I mind?' she shrugged with a pretence at indifference. But inwardly, she was cursing her father. Why do you have to interfere, Daddy? she gritted to herself. 'However,' she said aloud, 'I am a little surprised. After all, yesterday morning you told me you never wanted to see me again.'

'I'm going to see your father,' he reminded her drily, 'not you. Anyway, I've changed my mind, as it happens. I suppose I've got a sort of proprietorial interest in you—I might as well find out what happened to you in the end.'

'Charming!' she grinned savagely. He made her sound like a dog he had once owned. Jack Ford peered in through the doorway.

'I'm just about to leave, Ingrid——'

'It's all right, Jack,' she said. 'I've got a lift in after all. Thanks, anyway.'

'Right ho—see you tomorrow.'

Brendan watched him leave, then turned his

disturbing gaze back on to Ingrid.

'What's Marjorie doing tonight?' she asked sweetly. 'Swabbing the decks?'

'She's visiting some friends,' he told her coolly. His eyes were taking her in with calm interest. 'You've changed a great deal since I saw you last, Thursday Hunter. I trust you've had no after-effects of your amnesia?'

'None, thank you,' she answered coldly. He was considerably more elegant than he had been yesterday; his powerful frame looked devastating in a beautifully-cut leather sports jacket, and the dark blue silk scarf at the throat of his pinstriped shirt discreetly hid the exciting curls of dark hair which she knew would be visible otherwise. The latent savagery in him, the raw male power, was leashed tonight under the urbane veneer of fashion. For all that, Brendan radiated male sexuality effortlessly, and she could feel her own instincts swaying her towards him, urging her to reach out to him——

She stopped such dangerous thoughts brusquely, and tried to maintain her nonchalance.

'Had any business today?' she asked, shifting the conversation to neutral ground.

'Quite a bit,' he nodded. '*Southern Cross* is one of this year's best designs.'

'Your modesty is breathtaking,' she said sarcastically.

He shrugged.

'It's true—why should I lie about it? People are flocking to place orders. I've had firm requests for six already—which will keep the yard busy for the next year at least. So,' he grinned, 'I can afford to take the evening off.' He offered her his arm. 'Shall we go?'

As they walked to the car which he had hired, he glanced at her.

'Did you find out what became of your fiancé—what his name, Sam?'

'Tom,' she said stiffly. 'Yes, I found out. He simply went home—as you suggested.'

'And have you seen him since you got back?'

'Yes,' she said uncommunicatively. But Brendan refused to be put off by her grimness.

'And?' he demanded.

'And nothing,' she snapped. 'I went to see him—he nearly had heart failure!'

'Good,' he grinned, opening the door of the yellow Jaguar for her. As he inserted his big frame behind the wheel, he asked, 'And if it's not too personal a question—what's become of your engagement?'

'That's none of your business,' Ingrid retorted angrily.

'Don't be so pompous,' he chuckled. 'Aren't we old friends? So tell me, are you still engaged to Jim?'

'Tom,' she corrected furiously. 'And if you really want to know—yes, as it happens, I *am* engaged to him.'

'That's funny,' he said calmly, steering the car into the marine parade, 'your father told me you hadn't seen him for weeks.'

Flushing hotly, she glanced at him; but he was preoccupied with the traffic ahead, his face expressionless.

'Ah, the old country,' he said, looking up through the windscreen at the rainy sky, 'you can always rely on England for a bit of rain.' He smiled to himself. 'So it's all over between you and Tom, is it?' he asked.

Ingrid wrestled with her pride for a moment, then nodded unwillingly.

'Yes,' she sighed, 'it's all over.'

'Are you upset about it?' he asked casually.

'Why should I be?' she snapped, angered and disturbed by his interest in her private life.

'Weren't you crazy about him once?' he asked

reasonably. 'After all, you got engaged to him—he bought you that chain, remember?'

'I never loved Tom,' she said tautly. 'And I can't believe he ever loved me.'

'Oh?' He raised an eyebrow ironically. 'Then why did you get engaged to him?'

She sighed heavily, looking deep into her own heart for the answer to that question—a question which she had asked herself many times since her return to England.

'I suppose,' she said quietly, 'Tom was my symbol of rebellion. I chose him because he was so obviously unsuitable. Because I knew it would outrage Daddy. And getting engaged to him, in a way, helped me to identify with my own parents. I suppose I'd always resented my step-parents, no matter how loving they were, simply because they weren't my real parents; and I hated the way people said that my real father was such a crook. I guess planning to marry Tom—who was so obviously a selfish, dishonest person—made me feel closer to my real mother. I don't know how to explain it,' she said, suddenly acutely embarrassed. 'I've put it very badly, I'm afraid.'

'No,' Brendan said quietly, 'I think you've put it very well, Ingrid.' He glanced at her with assessing grey eyes. 'That was quite a good piece of self-analysis.'

'Well, don't sound so surprised,' she snapped bitterly. 'I'm not a complete moron, you know.'

'I never said you were,' he answered mildly.

'Your tone implied it.'

'Well, you have to admit that the Ingrid Marchant I said goodbye to in Hawaii would never have been capable of seeing herself so clearly,' he replied. She said nothing in reply, and he shrugged slightly to himself. 'So—when did you first realise that you weren't in love with Tom Maynard?'

'It wasn't a question of realising,' she retorted. 'I simply never was—and that's all.'

'How do you know?' He looked at her searchingly. 'Wouldn't you have gone on and married him?'

'Yes,' she replied, meeting his eyes, 'I would have married Tom. If I hadn't met you.'

A veil of ice descended over Brendan's eyes. And for the remainder of the hour's drive back into London, they were silent.

As she might have expected, had she given the matter any thought, Brendan and her stepfather got on well. Once the polite necessities had been dispensed with, they sat in the drawing-room, talking pleasantly, while Ingrid sat by, grim and silent.

Sir Geoffrey Marchant was obviously intrigued by this powerfully-built and self-assured man who had saved his daughter's life.

'Ingrid's never been particularly communicative about that whole episode,' the Rear-Admiral said, looking at Brendan critically. 'I'd like to hear the whole story, if I may—as you saw it, Mr Kavanagh.'

'Well——' Brendan glanced at Ingrid, whose face was scarcely encouraging, 'there's not all that much to tell, Sir Geoffrey.' He narrated the story simply and without adornment—leaving very little out. He did not disguise his own reluctance to take Ingrid on at first, nor did he minimise the quarrel they had had at Hawaii.

When he had done, the Rear-Admiral shook his head in amazement.

'Thursday Hunter, eh?' He reached out to take Ingrid's hand. 'You never told me it was that bad, child. Nor how kind Mr Kavanagh was to you.' He turned back to Brendan. 'My dear sir, you must stay to dinner—you'll have to take pot luck, I'm afraid, but——'

'I'm sure Mr Kavanagh has to get back to his friend,' Ingrid interrupted drily. 'You can't just abandon Miss Leppard, after all, can you?'

'Marjorie's staying with friends tonight,' Brendan answered calmly. 'I told you. And thank you, Sir Geoffrey—I should be delighted to stay to dinner.' He met Ingrid's savage glance with a mocking smile.

The evening turned out a delightfully pleasant one. Pleasant, that was, for Brendan and Sir Geoffrey Marchant; Ingrid was sulky and resentful, finding it impossible—or uncongenial—to share their obvious enjoyment of one anothers' company.

How thrilled she would have been, once, to have had Brendan here, at her father's table; and how proud she would have been to see the easy grace with which he got on with the crusty old Rear-Admiral. Yet now she hated the whole performance, knowing that Brendan was going back to Marjorie Leppard that night— knowing that he had snubbed her, despised her.

And when at last the evening was over, she was acutely relieved. Her stepfather had been regaling Brendan with the news that Ingrid had changed such a lot since her return from the Pacific, his ruddy face shining with pride; and she had been embarrassed beyond belief at his fatherly enthusiasm. It was wonderful to know that she and her stepfather had finally buried the hatchet, that he was at last proud of her—but it was also mortifying to be boasted about to a cynical man' whose mocking grey eyes across the table continually assured her of his real feelings towards her—amusement and scorn.

And what was more, her stepfather seemed to think he was showing considerable tact by not seeing Brendan to his car.

'Ingrid, you show Mr Kavanagh to his car. I'll get along up to bed, and let you say your goodbyes.' And shaking Brendan's hand, had closed the door firmly, leaving her to escort Brendan to the yellow Jaguar parked a little distance from the front door.

'That was a very pleasant evening,' he remarked mildly, as she walked stiffly by his side.

'Very,' she answered shortly.

'Your stepfather is a fascinating man.'

'Also an interfering one,' she replied as they reached the car. 'I'm sorry you had to come all this way—Daddy was only trying to be polite to you.'

'I've enjoyed it very much, Ingrid. I told you.' His eyes were dark and intent on hers. 'Meeting Sir Geoffrey has helped me to understand you a lot more.'

'How nice for you,' she said sweetly. 'You'd better hurry,' she added, looking pointedly at her watch. 'You don't want to keep Marjorie waiting. And it's a long drive back to Southampton.'

'I'm not going back to Southampton. I'm booked into Claridges, here in London.'

She looked at him sharply. 'On your own?' she asked, surprised. He looked at her with a lazy smile.

'On my own? Whatever gave you that idea? Marjorie and I are sharing a room, of course.'

'I see,' she said grimly, slightly shocked by his bald admission. He grinned.

'Don't sound so disapproving—it *is* done, you know.'

'Yes, of course it is,' she agreed flatly. 'Goodnight, Brendan.'

'Wait.' He was smiling as she turned to face him. 'What are you doing tomorrow night?'

'Tomorrow night?' she repeated in confusion. 'Nothing. But——'

'Excellent. Then you'll be free to come out with me.'

'I most certainly will *not*,' she retorted. 'I wouldn't go

out with you if you were the last man on earth!'

'Why not?'

'For one thing,' she said bitterly, 'I never go out with men who are already spoken for. And I don't care to cross swords with Marjorie Leppard.'

'You won't have to,' he told her silkily. 'Besides, your life belongs to me, remember? The least you can do is come and have a meal with me.'

'What for?' she asked angrily, her hands trembling. 'Are you going to try and add me to your harem?'

'I don't have a harem,' he said gently. 'And you once told me you were old-fashioned enough not to sleep with anyone. Except your husband, that is.'

'Brendan, I——'

'I'll see you tomorrow night, then,' he said firmly. 'I'll pick you up at seven-thirty. Sleep well.'

'I'm not going anywhere with you!' she yelped as he slid calmly behind the wheel. 'Don't you dare come——'

But he was already driving off, the street lights glinting golden off the roof of the yellow car.

CHAPTER NINE

'ARE you very much in love with him?'

Ingrid looked up in astonishment at her stepfather as she closed the heavy front door behind her.

'Wh-what?'

'I'm afraid it's painfully obvious,' the Rear-Admiral smiled gently, coming up to take her hand.

She looked at him, stunned.

'But I hate him, Daddy, I——' Her words stumbled to a halt as the realisation struck her. Of course she loved him! She had loved him for weeks, loved him perhaps ever since those terrible days on Fiji, when he was the only stable thing in an utterly lonely world. The knowledge of her own feelings for Brendan made her suddenly weak at the knees, and she leaned against her stepfather as he led her quietly into the sitting-room, where she sat down weakly in an armchair.

'Yes,' she whispered, her voice so soft that he could barely hear her. 'I'm so in love with him that it makes me ache, Daddy.'

He patted her head quietly, moved by her expression.

'I can't tell you how pleased I am for you, Ingrid,' he said gently. 'I couldn't think of a better man for you than Brendan Kavanagh——'

'You don't understand,' she said wryly, looking up at him with a twisted smile. 'He doesn't love me. He never will.'

'What makes you say that?'

'For one thing,' she said bitterly, 'he's already got a lover—a woman called Marjorie Leppard, who sailed with him from Australia. For another thing—well, he despises me, I'm afraid.' The sheen of tears in her beautiful green eyes made them glow like misty emeralds. 'Brendan Kavanagh isn't one to suffer fools gladly. And he thinks I'm a fool. And personally, I'm inclined to agree with his judgment.' She looked into the embers of the fire, biting back her tears.

'I think you've misjudged him, child,' Sir Geoffrey said calmly, still stroking her golden head. 'Dear me, how I wish Marcia were still alive—she'd know what to do, what to say.' He raised her head and peered at her in concern. 'I don't think he despises you, Ingrid,' he said firmly. 'On the contrary, I think he respects you greatly.'

'Respects?' She smiled slightly. 'I've done very little to make him respect me, Daddy.'

'When he spoke to me on the phone this morning, he was full of your praises,' he told her, his eyes thoughtful. 'He said what a pleasure it had been to meet you again, asked endless questions about you. That doesn't sound like the behaviour of a man who despises you, child.' She bit her lip, unwilling to entertain the hope that Brendan might, after all, have some pleasant feelings towards her, and her stepfather went on, 'As for this Marjorie Leppard—well, if he really feels anything for you, Ingrid, I doubt very much whether he can be as involved with her as you seem to think.'

'I'd like to believe you,' she said in a taut voice, 'but I daren't. Oh, Daddy, I love him so much! I'm so afraid that he'll leave me——'

'Is there any danger of that?' he asked gently. 'After all, you're going to be seeing him at Southampton every day for the next four days, aren't you? There'll be plenty of time to talk things over.'

'He's invited me out tomorrow night,' she said hesitantly. 'I told him I wouldn't go, but——'

'Oh, nonsense,' he retorted. 'Of course you'll go!

Why, that just proves my point. Of course he's interested in you. And if I know anything about women—men, too, come to think of it—it won't take you long to change his interest into something more permanent!'

He tugged her to her feet, his rugged face breaking into a happy smile, 'I don't know what you can be thinking of,' he reproached her, 'taking such a defeatist attitude! You're my daughter, Ingrid, and you're going to go out there and do your best. Whether you win or lose,' he nodded, 'you're going to do your level best!'

The next day dawned bright and clear for the first time in weeks, and the brilliant sunshine brought droves of people flocking to Southampton for the Show, making it one of the busiest days in the history of the Boat Show. Ingrid did not see Brendan at all during the day and at her request, Plum Wright let her get home early, giving her an hour or two to prepare in.

She had long since decided on the dress she was going to wear, and as she tried it on in front of her dressing-table mirror, she studied herself with mounting excitement. The dress was formal in one sense, having a billowing taffeta skirt which reached to the ground; in all other senses, though, it was extravagantly beautiful—and voluptuous. The deep rose silk contrasted stunningly with the light gold of her skin; but it was the collar which took the eye most. It plunged from high ruffles that framed her exquisite oval face to a deep neckline which flattered the full curve of her breasts. She had pinned a satin rose of the same deep red colour to the breast, and the flower-like, almost Baroque curves of the ruffled collar closed excitingly just where her tan ended and the white swell of her breasts began.

She looked ravishing—and for all the perfection of her ardent youth, she also looked mature, poised, sophisticated. Only a few months ago, she reflected, she could never have carried off a dress like this one. It had been hanging in her closet for months, waiting for her to grow into it. Well, now she was ready for it. The deep rose silk rustled sensuously around her as she went to her jewellery box and took out the only diamonds she had, a pair of glittering earrings which her father had bought for her on her eighteenth birthday. The stones blazed like stars among the silky gold tresses of her hair, and she studied her reflection critically.

She was beautiful, yes. She would never, in all probability, look better than she did now; yet the knot of anxiety in her stomach prevented her from revelling in her appearance, or feeling the vanity which another woman might have enjoyed.

No other jewellery, she decided; and her beautiful skin would need very little make-up—just a darkening of mascara on her lashes, a touch of eye-shadow, a delicate touch of shine on her mouth.

What did the evening hold? She did not dare think, did not dare hope that she would receive more than a bit of gentle mockery from Brendan. She had been disappointed too sharply and too often to dare expect anything. The clear evening was cool, and she slipped her exquisitely soft fur cape, made of shadow fox, over her shoulders before turning out the light, and rustling downstairs to wait for Brendan.

The Rear-Admiral looked up as she came in, and his words of greeting tailed off as he stared at her wide-eyed.

'Is it too much?' she asked in sudden worry. 'Should I change into something more formal?'

'Ingrid, you look ravishing,' he said, shaking his head in wonder. He walked round her, his normally stern features softened with wonder and delight. 'You're so very lovely, my dear child—I've never dreamed you could look like this!' He kissed her gently on the cheek, and then held her at arm's length to study her. 'I wish Marcia were alive now,' he said quietly, 'to see her daughter like this . . .'

They embraced quickly, both too moved to want to say more. Instead they sat quietly, reminiscing about her childhood, until the chime of the doorbell, announcing Brendan's arrival, sent butterflies whirling through her stomach. Sir Geoffrey opened the door to him, and ushered him in—a magnificent figure in full evening dress. Ingrid rose to greet him, more nervous than she had ever been, and was rewarded by the light in his deep grey eyes as he took her in.

'You look wonderful,' he said simply, his authoritative mouth curving into a quiet smile. 'I knew you would.'

But a little while later, as they drove off down the street in his Jaguar, he glanced at her with a wry smile.

'I was half expecting you not to come,' he confessed. 'After what you said last night, I had the feeling you might have gone out with someone else—just to spite me.'

'No,' she said gently, 'there's no one else, Brendan.' The inner meaning of her words did not seem to reach him, however, and he merely nodded.

It was a beautiful autumn evening, the sky fading rose and salmon-pink overhead as he drove down through the centre of London, along the Caledonian Road through King's Cross to the eighteenth-century elegance of Clerkenwell and Holborn, then towards the riverside.

'Where are we going?' she wanted to know.

'We're having dinner on a floating restaurant,' he told her with a secret smile. They had reached Blackfriars, and the expanse of the Thames, a silver sweep of water in the evening purple, was visible ahead.

As he drove across Blackfriars Bridge, she noticed that there was a tall yacht moored on the far side of the bank, opposite the last resting place of Captain Scott's famous *Discovery*. The utter elegance of the boat's lines proclaimed her to be one of the last of the nineteenth-century clippers.

'That's odd,' she said, looking at the schooner in puzzlement, 'I never noticed that boat there before. I wonder if she's a new floating museum?'

'Museum?' he snorted, amused. 'Everything on her's in perfect working order, I assure you. That's *Whiplash*.'

It took a few seconds for his words to sink in, and then she blinked in astonishment.

'*Whiplash*? Your schooner—the one you were going to buy in Los Angeles?' He nodded, his eyes amused. 'But—but——' she spluttered at him, 'how did she *get* here?'

'I sailed her here, of course,' he said casually, driving along Bankside to where the beautiful masts reached up into the dying sun.

'But you sailed your other boat here—*Southern Cross*, the one you're exhibiting at Southampton!'

'No,' he said. 'My colleague, Joe Prince, sailed *Southern Cross*.'

She was still bewildered. 'But you said Marjorie had helped you sail *Southern Cross*——'

'No, I didn't,' he corrected her with a grin. 'That's what you thought you heard. I said Marje had helped sail *Southern Cross* from Sydney. She did—she helped Joe Prince sail her. I was following in *Whiplash*.' He parked the car, and led Ingrid, still stunned as she was, to the magnificent yacht. 'There, didn't I tell you she was one of the most beautiful things in the world?'

Clinging to Brendan's hand, she gazed up at the rakish lines of the schooner. She was a big boat, well over fifty feet long, and she had been built out of teak and mahogany, with the loving skill of a bygone era. 'She was designed in 1884,' Brendan said softly. 'She's the sweetest thing afloat, Ingrid—and you're going to love her.'

'I'm still a bit puzzled,' she said, shaking her head at him, 'but I agree—she is very lovely. You're very lucky to have her.'

'Ah,' he said with a smile, 'but she's not mine. I'm giving her to someone else.'

Before she had a chance to ask him what he meant, he was escorting her up the gangplank and on to the wide deck of the beautiful old schooner.

'Is this what you meant by a floating restaurant?' she asked him, as he led her down into the stateroom.

'I'm afraid so,' he nodded. 'Are you disappointed?'

Her gasp of awe answered him as she stepped into the massive stateroom. It was more like something from the great age of ocean liners than a room on a private yacht. The velvety carpet underfoot was as luxurious as the heavy brocade curtains at the wide windows. The soft light of the chandelier overhead, supplemented by coach-lamps on the bulkheads, gleamed softly on furnishings of maple, mahogany, and satinwood. To her amazement, the bulkheads themselves had been moulded and gilded, and a large and beautiful seascape in oils was framed against the far end of the room.

'They knew how to build boats in those days,' said Brendan with a slight smile on his beautiful mouth. 'Let me take your cape.'

Wordlessly, she let him take the fur off her shoulders, and walked forward in a daze, taking in the magnificence of the fittings. Despite the utter luxury of the long cabin, she could see that it was perfectly seaworthy, too. The fine furniture had been firmly bolted to the deck, and velvet cushioning along the bulkheads and on the edges of all the furniture would protect against bumps in heavy weather. As if reading her thoughts, Brendan nodded.

'She's one of the safest sailing boats afloat. And it takes very heavy weather indeed to make her pitch at all.'

'Oh, Brendan,' she sighed, turning to him with shining eyes, 'she's absolutely beautiful! I've never seen anything like her!' He looked into her eyes with a strange half-smile—an expression she had seen once before on his face, and one which made her insides melt. He took her slender hand silently, and raised it to his lips, kissing her fingers softly.

'Come,' he murmured, 'let's sit by the window and have a drink before we start dinner.'

'You've made dinner?' she queried, still shaken by the intensity of the expression in his eyes. 'On board *Whiplash*?'

'Of course. After all, I owe you at least one splendid shipboard meal—remember?' He led her to the velvet sofa by one of the wide windows, and went to a silver-railed sideboard to pour them both a whisky. 'I'm afraid I was telling an untruth when I said I was booked into Claridges. As a matter of fact, I've been staying here—on board *Whiplash*. I had to get special permission to moor her here, of course.'

Ingrid watched his powerful, elegant figure as he poured the drinks and brought them over, her heart in her mouth.

'And Marjorie?' she whispered. 'Isn't she—isn't she staying with you?'

'Marje is my cousin,' he told her, clinking his glass gravely against hers. 'She's also engaged to a very large young man called Cass, whom she loves very much.'

'I thought——'

'You thought wrong,' he purred. He watched her

with deep, wise eyes over the rim of his glass as he drank, and then leaned back to survey her. 'You're so very beautiful,' he said in his velvety, deep voice. 'A midnight-blue voice, she had once thought it—and thought so still. 'You're like a queen in that dress, Thursday Hunter. And you're like a queen stark naked, too.'

The colour rushed to her cheeks, and she dropped her emerald eyes, toying with the rose at her breast. The distant sound of a ship's siren drifted along the river towards them in the silence.

'I couldn't stay away from you,' Brendan said softly, and she looked up at him, her heart pounding. He took her glass out of her nerveless fingers, put it on the table, and pulled her against his chest.

With a rustle of silk she was in his arms, hugging his strength to her, her face buried in his neck. His words were soft and gentle, dropping into her soul like balm.

'I tried to forget you, Ingrid.' His hand stroked the golden sheen of her hair quietly. 'I tried so very hard to put you out of my mind—telling myself you were too young for me, too immature. I tried to remind myself of how inexperienced you were, how innocent. I even tried to believe that you belonged to a different generation— that I was far too old for you. But it wasn't true. And it didn't work.'

She clung to him, not trusting herself to speak, and he kissed her tenderly on the satiny skin of her neck, her cheeks, the trembling corner of her mouth.

'I love you, Ingrid—so very much that I don't know how to begin telling you. Since I left you in Hawaii, I've done nothing but dream about you—and curse myself for letting you slip out of my arms.'

'Oh, darling,' she whispered tearfully, 'I've loved you for weeks and months—and I've dreamed about you, too——'

His lips silenced her roughly as his kiss brought the sweet, hot memories rushing back to her, making her press the soft contours of her body against his hard male power.

'I didn't know what made me bring *Whiplash* to England,' he said when he had released her mouth. 'I just knew I had to, that's all. She was a difficult boat to sail single-handed—she really needs a crew of two—and on the long, lonely voyage, I'd almost persuaded myself that I'd got you out of my system. I think I would still have come to see you,' he smiled tenderly, caressing her lips with his own, 'but I'd just about persuaded my stupid self that you were too young and immature for me.' Once again, their mouths locked in a kiss that was fathoms deep in passion.

'If only you knew,' Ingrid said tremulously, 'I've been doing exactly the same thing—trying to convince myself that we weren't suited. What made us fight against this, Brendan?'

'God alone knows,' he purred, his lips devouring the scented hollow of her throat as she clung to him joyfully. They looked into each other's eyes, drowning in the love that had suddenly overflowed in them.

'When you arrived on the jetty next to *Southern Cross*, I thought my heart had stopped,' he told her. 'The hardest thing I've ever done was to send you away then. God, how stupid and cruel I was—and it nearly broke my own heart to wound you!'

'I thought you hated me,' she cried, 'I thought you and Marjorie were——'

'I'd instructed Marjorie to cling on to me like that if ever we should meet you,' he confessed. 'She was very upset afterwards, once she'd seen how much we'd hurt you. My only thought had been to prevent you from getting any ideas about me—but afterwards, Marje gave me hell.' He grinned ruefully. 'She called me every kind of fool and cad for rebuffing you like that—and half-way through, I began to realise what my true feelings were about you. I didn't sleep much that night. And the next morning, I just had to phone your father.'

'You told me that *he* phoned *you*,' she protested.

'I didn't want you getting any big ideas yet,' he smiled. 'Anyway, when your father told me how much you'd suffered, how changed you were, I knew that I didn't have the slightest excuse for staying away any longer. And by then you were cold and distant with me.'

'Only trying to protect myself,' she said, pressing her face against his and hugging him close. 'Oh, it's so good to feel you close to me again, Brendan! I think I'd have died without you.'

'And I without you,' he said quietly. 'We're going to be very happy together, Ingrid—but we'd have been so very unhappy apart.'

A long kiss later, she looked up at him with dewy eyes, her pulses racing.

'I don't want dinner,' she said huskily. 'Is there a double bed in the captain's cabin?'

His delighted laughter made her hang her head in blushing confusion.

'You little wanton,' he murmured, still rocking with amusement, 'didn't you tell me that you were old-fashioned enough to want to be married first?'

She looked up at him with intoxicating green eyes, the perfection of her mouth inviting his kiss.

'I'd come to you anyhow you wanted me, Brendan,' she said softly, and the smile faded from his eyes, to be replaced with a passionate, desiring love that made her want to melt into his arms.

'I believe you would,' he said with that strange half-smile. 'I believe you would. But we're going to do things the old-fashioned way, my darling one—there's too much wickedness in this wicked world already!'

Ingrid gurgled with laughter, divinely contented, and reached out slender fingers to caress that magnificent face, the face that had haunted her dreams for so long.

'You're so perfect that it frightens me,' she whispered, and he held her close.

'Don't ever leave me,' he groaned. 'I need you so much, Ingrid. I've needed you, loved you, ever since you first opened those green witch's eyes on board *Seaspray*. And the first time I realised how deeply I felt about you was that day with the dolphins. It was then I began to realise that the rest of my life was going to be a desert without you.'

'It nearly broke my heart to leave you,' she confessed. 'You were so stern with me, so harsh——'

'I had to be. Do you remember how I told you once that you frightened me because of the responsibility you represented?' She nodded silently. 'I didn't want to get involved with you, darling. All my life I've tried to avoid being responsible for anyone else—unconsciously, I couldn't bear the hurt of being left alone again.' Again, she nodded, understanding shining in her eyes. 'Well, on board *Seaspray* I knew I was falling in love with you—and God knows how I fought against it. I knew that the girl I fell in love with could disappear any second, like a puff of smoke. As soon as your memory returned, I knew that things between us would be over.'

'But they weren't,' she protested, clinging to him.

'No,' he smiled, 'they weren't. But I thought they were—especially when it seemed that you were still infatuated with Tom Maynard.' He silenced her protestations with a kiss. 'And when you'd gone,' he continued, 'I was burning up with jealousy and loneliness. God, I was so miserable! I called myself every kind of a fool for having allowed myself to fall in love with you—for having exposed myself to that kind of pain. And that made me harsh, even cruel.'

'But it's all turned out all right, hasn't it?' Ingrid asked urgently, distraught at the memory of the hurt in his eyes.

'Oh, darling,' he said gently, 'you don't need to ask that.'

'Kiss me again,' she pleaded, her shining lips parted for him, unable to bear not touching him. Brendan smiled softly, obeying her with a tenderness that made her shudder all over.

'I'm afraid I don't happen to have a ring in my pocket,' he said afterwards. 'But I realised at last why I'd bought *Whiplash* to England. She's your wedding present, darling. If you marry me, that is.'

'If?' she whispered. 'Oh, sweet man, how can you even ask?'

'It's always best to ask,' he grinned. 'Now—I think that dinner ought to be ready by now. My plan is to have it here—with a bottle of Krug, of course——'

'Of course,' she smiled, her eyes brimming with happiness.

'—and then to weigh anchor, and sail down the Thames to the sea.'

'And then?' she whispered.

'And then I'm going to show you the double bed in the captain's cabin,' he purred.

Once again, her mouth was buried in his, her heart fluttering as wildly as a trapped bird as his hands pressed her body against his hard power.

'You know,' he said, low and soft against her ear, 'Ingrid is a beautiful name. But in my heart of hearts— and even when you're the mother of my children—I shall always think of you as—Thursday Hunter.'

And then there were no more thoughts, no more separation, nothing except the sweet flame that was making them into one glorious blaze of joy.

APHRODITE, GODDESS OF LOVE

Aphrodite was the ancient Greek goddess of love and beauty. Some said that her father was Zeus, the king of the gods. Others believed that she simply sprang from the foam of the sea.

The Romans called her Venus, and the most famous artistic rendition of her is the *Venus de Milo*, a great statue in the Louvre museum.

Aphrodite is pictured in many other artworks. Always she is beautiful, but she is depicted in different ways. In some paintings, she is the goddess of pure love. In others, she is the goddess of marriage and family life. Often you will see paintings of Aphrodite against backgrounds of storms and lightning, indicating her tumultuous passions. Yet she is also associated with the dove, the sparrow, the swallow and the swan, symbols of peace and gentle affection.

It is said that Aphrodite possessed a magic girdle, which made her irresistibly desirable and gave her the power to make the gods fall in love with her.

As for her own desires, she was married to Hephaestus (Vulcan in Roman mythology), the god of fire. But she had a passion for mortal men, particularly the handsome Adonis. When Adonis was killed by a boar, Aphrodite made the red anemone flower grow from his blood.

Aphrodite plays an important part in many legends and stories. She gave beauty as a gift to Pandora, the first woman. She caused the Trojan War, siding with the Trojans against the Greeks. And over the ages her name has inspired numerous poems and works of prose, including the book you hold in your hands.

Take these
4 best-selling novels
FREE

Yes! Four sophisticated, contemporary love stories by four world-famous authors of romance FREE, as your introduction to the Harlequin Presents subscription plan. Thrill to **Anne Mather**'s passionate story BORN OUT OF LOVE, set in the Caribbean.... Travel to darkest Africa in **Violet Winspear**'s TIME OF THE TEMPTRESS....Let **Charlotte Lamb** take you to the fascinating world of London's Fleet Street in MAN'S WORLD .... Discover beautiful Greece in **Sally Wentworth**'s moving romance SAY HELLO TO YESTERDAY.

Harlequin Presents...

The very finest in romance fiction

Join the millions of avid Harlequin readers all over the world who delight in the magic of a really exciting novel. EIGHT great NEW titles published EACH MONTH! Each month you will get to know exciting, interesting, true-to-life people .... You'll be swept to distant lands you've dreamed of visiting .... Intrigue, adventure, romance, and the destiny of many lives will thrill you through each Harlequin Presents novel.

Get all the latest books before they're sold out!
As a Harlequin subscriber you actually receive your personal copies of the latest Presents novels immediately after they come off the press, so you're sure of getting all 8 each month.

Cancel your subscription whenever you wish!
You don't have to buy any minimum number of books. Whenever you decide to stop your subscription just let us know and we'll cancel all further shipments.